9.75

2-16-72

MASOUD THE BEDOUIN

Bedouin Sheikh

MASOUD
THE BEDOUIN

BY

ALFREDA POST CARHART

ILLUSTRATED   BY
JESSIE   GILLESPIE

BOOKS FOR LIBRARIES PRESS
FREEPORT, NEW YORK

First Published 1915
Reprinted 1971

INTERNATIONAL STANDARD BOOK NUMBER:
0-8369-3838-0

LIBRARY OF CONGRESS CATALOG CARD NUMBER:
76-150541

PRINTED IN THE UNITED STATES OF AMERICA

To the People whom I Love
Whose Land was my Birthplace
Whose Homes were ever open to Me
To my Friends the Syrians
This Little Book
Is Affectionately Inscribed

CONTENTS

ILLUSTRATIONS

PREFACE

THOUGH the following stories are presented as fiction, almost all the incidents portrayed have actually occurred in various parts of Syria. The sayings of the different characters are literal translations from familiar Arabic speech, and the customs depicted are those known only through intimate mingling with that ever-fascinating life of the East.

It should be borne in mind that there is no one type of Syrian life,—each district, each religious sect, having its distinctive features. Syria is, in fact, an epitome of history, preserving in crystallized form in its various regions the life and customs of the main epochs of past time.

The earliest form of half-civilized life is the patriarchal and pastoral. This is preserved in its most romantic form among the Bedouins. They use goat's-hair tents, lead their flocks about, and entertain strangers, much as Abraham did, and indulge in the same raids for plunder that the Amalekites and Midianites waged of old, but observing always a code of chivalry and honor which regulates even robbery and murder.

The next type of development is preserved in the agricultural village life of the interior, of the same class as the life depicted in the book of Judges. A group of flat-roofed, windowless abodes, huddled together as closely as possible for safety, is the home of a simple, brave-hearted community, who cultivate their scanty fields and reap their harvests under the risk of attack from desert raids, as in the days of Gideon, while the women carry their jars to the fountain as did Rebecca and Rachel at a still earlier time.

We advance a step higher in civilization to the cities of the interior, with their narrow, vaulted streets, crowded market-places, primitive courts of justice, and secluded housetops. Not very different were Jerusalem and Samaria in the days of the Kings.

We move forward further in the march of time, passing by the relics of ancient empires —ruined temples and hid treasure—to the event which focalizes all history, making this beautiful Syria unique among all lands as the birthplace of Jesus. Here we still find the descendants of the early Christian Church. Much has been added since to the simple belief of the Fathers, much of superstition and form, but there remains the foundation upon which the faith has stood in face of persecution these many centuries.

We hurry on through the changes of history to the overwhelming event of the Middle Ages, the Moslem invasion. Here the religion of the Prophet prevailed against a vitiated Christianity and here it still holds the dominant power, with its ceremonial prayers, its fasts, its vows, and its system of social seclusion which has influenced all other types of life in the East.

Lastly, we come to a seeming incongruity—the twentieth century civilization—which is pouring its good and its evil into the seacoast towns and thence into all parts of the land. The railroad and carriage roads of Lebanon now compete with the patient, loaded camel; well-built, healthful houses are fast supplanting the old dingy huts; the peasant woman now fills her jar from a finely constructed fountain of carved stone; and the city shopkeeper looks out from his tiny booth upon fashionable equip-ages, extreme Parisian costumes, and, across the street, the drinking and gambling saloon.

But there are better things coming into Syria from the lands of the West. The life-giving impulse of Christianity, which nearly two thousand years ago started from Syrian shores, is now brought back by the missionaries to the land of its birth in the form of a system of education, a simple worship, and above all, a Book. All over the Syria of to-day are vitalized Christian homes. Simple churches and schools, scattered over Lebanon, have become as ensigns upon the mountains; while, in the city, schools of higher grade and a great college strive to give with the education that the ambitious young people of the land are now determined to have, the dynamic of a spiritual religion.

Prominence has not, however, been given in these pages to the more cultured type of Syrian life, as it is similar to life with which we are familiar. We have dwelt rather upon the ruder and bolder conditions of the East, upon those customs which are passing away, to which the Syrians of the future will look back with pride as the steps upon which they rose to the higher life.

Many of the incidents of the wilder life of Bedouins and remote villages were furnished by Prof. J. Stewart Crawford of the Syrian Protestant College of Beirut, and the late Rev. William K. Eddy, the beloved missionary of Sidon.

The author wishes to express hearty thanks to Miss Jessie Gillespie Willing for her labor of love in drawing the pen and ink illustrations.

The photographs reproduced were in the main taken by Mons. Bonfils of Beirut.

Thanks are due to the *Independent, Christian Herald, Congregationalist, Observer, Interior, Christian Messenger,* Woman's Presbyterian Board and *Packer Alumna,* for the privilege of reprinting those of the stories that were first published by them.

ALFREDA POST CARHART

BEIRUT, SYRIA
      April 15, 1915.

THE WAY OF THEM THAT DWELL IN TENTS

Tent Dwellers

I

MASOUD THE BEDOUIN

THE level rays of sunset burned red upon the huts of Banias, the modern Cæsarea Philippi. Here and there a low beam struggled through the shrubbery, and struck like a reflection of past glory upon the base of some ancient column built in with the irregular stones of a modern wall. It was summer-time, and the population had crept out of their unspeakably dingy, windowless abodes, and had built themselves booths of leaves upon the flat housetops. The village appeared to be keeping the Feast of Tabernacles.

Upon one of the roofs stood a figure that might have been worked in bronze, so motionless and bold it stood against the golden-red sky. Two ropelike black cords bound the

1

heavy folds of head-drapery over a brow set with some deep purpose. The hand grasped one of the daggers at the belt. The man's eyes followed contemptuously the curvets of a horseman upon the plain below. The rider had acquired to perfection the Oriental ideal of action in horsemanship. He leaned forward in his saddle, draperies fluttering, lance uplifted, and outstretched elbows flourishing wildly, in time with every bound of the horse. The man of bronze muttered to himself:

"Fool! Do you think that one small year can wipe your treachery from my memory? Take your pleasure now! You will never ride beyond these hills."

It was a bitter wrong that had caused such bitter hatred. A year before, this dark-faced Masoud was to have married the most piquant, sparkling-eyed brunette in the region. He had courted her according to a quaint usage, spending an evening solemnly smoking the argileh with her father, and, on parting, leaving behind him, as though by accident, his "token." The custom is well understood: if the father wishes to accept the suitor, he keeps the token; if not, he returns it. In Masoud's case, the token was a small wallet of antique design. Aniseh's father had picked it up in some disdain;— should he give his bright-eyed daughter to a roving Bedouin?

But Aniseh was not the usual meek Oriental girl, grateful to have her life molded for her. She put her two hands upon the token, and poutingly asked:

"Why return it? Don't you think you might hurt his feelings?"

The idea seemed too ludicrous to allow a proper show of anger. With those shy brown eyes raised to his, the father could not bring himself to loosen the slender fingers, and the wallet was never returned.

Masoud became almost gentle after this, until one fated day. During his absence on a raid, as Aniseh and her companions were gaily carrying their jars to the fountain, they were attacked by three horsemen, and Aniseh was snatched away. The leader was a Bedouin known throughout the region as Khalil the Cunning, and his companions were his two younger brothers, his apprentices in deeds of treachery.

The news of the capture reached the tent of

Masoud's mother like a message of doom and she waited in agony at the thought of her son's rage. At sunset, two days later, she was crouching at the door of the hair-cloth tent, trying with wrinkled, tattooed lips, to blow a charcoal fire into a blaze. She half raised herself to draw breath, when she caught sight of his set face, more terrible than the rage that she was expecting. He made a sign for her to keep silent, and asked,

"Where is my brother?"

In answer a young man appeared at the tent door. Masoud turned to him:

"If you value the family honor, go to Khalil and say, 'Masoud warns you.'"

The young man drew together the fingertips of his right hand with a singular gesture implying "Trust me," and disappeared down the darkening valley.

Masoud spent the night on the rocky hillside. His devotion to the ancient Bedouin rules of honor forbade his attacking Khalil unwarned; his equal firmness in the Bedouin principles of revenge made certain Khalil's doom.

After that time Masoud lived a weird, half-goblin life, now in Bashan, now in Palmyra, appearing suddenly, vanishing strangely, always watching for a trace of his wary enemy.

At last he decided upon a new course. It was after a fruitless attempt to trace Khalil in one of the Lebanon villages. Masoud was leaning against a wall, gazing absently upon the ground, when his eye fell upon the open lid of a ground-spider's den, the hairy creature himself dragging his prey through the opening. The fairy-built door closed upon them both struggling. Masoud's eyes gleamed darkly.

"You have taught me how," he breathed through clenched teeth. "I shall watch for my enemy like the monster of the ground; he will not see me till he falls into my clutches."

And thus it was that Masoud had been lurking among the huts of Banias, rarely seen except by the old man whose cattle he tended. The ruse was a wise one. Khalil, ever light-headed, had ceased to realize the perseverance of his enemy and was returning at last to inspect some of his flocks and herds in the Hermon district.

When Masoud had assured himself who the

dashing rider was, he lost no time in reaching the ground, opening the rickety door of the hut, and drawing out from a heap of brush-wood a revolver and a battle-ax, which he added to the armament in his belt. A shepherd's coat thrown over his shoulders covered all.

He went first to the market-place and accosted a certain horse dealer with the usual greetings, receiving the usual replies.

"May your evening be fortunate."

"May yours be blessed."

"How is your health?"

"Praise be to Allah!"

"I hope you are well."

"Under your oversight."

"Under the oversight of Allah."

Then came the real question.

"Who is riding your red horse down in the plain?"

"What! have you not heard that Khalil the Cunning has just arrived? His horse was nearly dead, so he is trying my red one. He will be back soon."

Masoud slipped back among the bystanders and soon stole away behind a wall.

In a short time the rider appeared, and flung himself down from the saddle with much clanking of weapons. He threw the reins to the dealer, exclaiming:

"The brute! Curse the religion of his harim! He stumbles, and loses wind, and makes no speed at all."

Masoud, from his hiding-place, smiled grimly, as he thought of the curvets that he had watched. Khalil had evidently never taken such satisfaction in a horse.

Khalil ran his hand down the horse's fetlocks, criticizing him at every point. The dealer loudly attested his excellence by the virtue of his own religion, by his father's, his grandfather's, and his great-grandfather's.

"Let me see the pedigree once more," said Khalil.

A greasy document was produced, signed with many seals. Khalil did not question the statements on the paper, as he had done with all the spoken assertions of the dealer. It is understood that, though a Bedouin may lie on every other subject, he will speak the truth in two matters: the blood that he has shed, and the pedigree of a horse.

Khalil looked at the dealer keenly.

"Now between you and me, what is your last price?"

With exquisite deference, the dealer replied:

"What need have we to consider such questions? I wish the Afendeh Khalil to honor me by accepting the horse as a gift."

Khalil answered, "I depend for all the good things of life upon your bounty. But what is your price?"

The man hesitated.

"If it were any one except your honorable presence, I should be disgracing myself by asking less than sixty Turkish liras, but for the sake of the love between us, I will ask for only fifty."

"May your eyes bury my heart, you dog!" said Khalil, "I'll give you fifteen."

"Do you wish me to starve my family? Do you wish me to cut my own throat? By the religion of my grandfather's beard——"

And so the tiresome haggling went on, and the two prices were brought gradually nearer to each other. But the meeting-place was not reached. Khalil started toward the khan where he was to spend the night.

"I shall start before light, if the Almighty wills, to meet my two brothers at Ain Balata. Follow me there during the day, and let us together inspect the horse."

A flame of wild joy, kindled in Gehenna itself, leaped in the heart of the dark man in the shadow. Like the famous scorpions of the place, he crept away behind the walls and held his sting in readiness.

Long before dawn he lay behind a rock on the road to Ain Balata, beside a sluggish rill which crept into a swamp. He had planned well. After about two hours a rider picked his way down the path, and stopped at the rill to water his horse. He was taking off the bit, when a creature like a fiend seized his right arm and thrust a dagger deep into his side. The frenzied man dragged him over the stones to a place where the morass suddenly deepened. Masoud braced himself upon a rock, and dragged his burden into the ooze. For one minute he held the weakly struggling man above the surface.

"Do you see me? Me? Do you see who has brought you to the slime where you belong?"

Then the unrelenting grasp pressed him

down, and Khalil sank forever into his miserable grave.

Nothing was now too reckless for Masoud. He stumbled his way back to the rill and found Khalil's horse still cropping the rare bit of grass that marks the path of a Syrian watercourse. He sprang into the saddle, and headed for Ain Balata.

"His brothers will be waiting for him," he said to himself. He was not disappointed. Before he reached the place, the two young men had recognized their brother's horse, and had started on foot to meet him. Masoud took a careful aim at the older one, and fired. The man fell instantly. Masoud dug his sharp-edged stirrups into his horse's flanks and rode down upon the younger brother, who was running to make his escape. He was a boy of seventeen and carried no firearms; he could merely plead for mercy.

"I shall not kill you," said Masoud, "you were too young to know what you were doing. But I mean to keep you from informing against me."

With that he tore off part of the boy's head drapery and gagged him; then stripped him of his tightly wound money-girdle and bound him with it to a secluded rock.

Masoud turned to escape. To his horror, the other victim was gone! Strange, in that open region, and a wounded man at that! Masoud remounted the horse and hunted all the low hills about—in vain. None but a Bedouin can elude a Bedouin, and here Masoud had found his equal. He did not discover the snakelike path which the wounded man took, up among the foot-hills, around the sweep of the plain, across to the Banias ravine, and up the hillside to the Crusaders' Castle. He did not see the poor fellow, almost spent, creep into a secret passage under the ruins; nor did he know when this brother of Khalil's, in darkness and alone, breathed his last. Years after, a traveler of more than usual curiosity was exploring the remoter parts of the castle, when his candle flickered upon the murdered man's skeleton. But no one else ever knew.

Masoud turned back in a rage from his fruitless search.

"It is dangerous," he thought, "to leave the child to betray me."

He retraced his steps to the rock, and shot the boy through the heart.

Years passed, during which Masoud took refuge first with one tribe, then with another, to elude the avengers of blood from Khalil's tribe.

One evening his encampment was set on a small table-land high on Lebanon. No living beings were in sight except a herd of gazelles, that sped over the hilltops before the outriders were in range. An unsuspected covey of partridges watched the newcomers with more assurance. Their sentinel stood above them on a rock that blended perfectly with his own drab-colored plumage, and eyed the riders as they picketed their horses. Not until the whole company arrived did he give his low warning cry, to send the covey scuttling away among the rocks. Partridges are quite too wary to fly in danger. The wild creatures of Syria, the bears, the gazelles, the partridges, know well why their Creator has dressed them in the subdued tints of their own soil, and they can hide themselves in an open country so as to escape every eye.

But the camp was too busy to think of game
just now. The patient women were carrying
burdens and setting up tents under the super-
vision of their lords. They must also prepare
the argilehs for their husbands to smoke, and
hurry with the supper; it was all done with
wonderful quickness. The camp-fires were
soon throwing flashes of color upon the
swarthy figures gathered round. One by one
the men muffled themselves in their sheepskin
coats, and went to sleep on the ground. No
sound remained except the stamping of the
horses, as they tried in vain to keep themselves
warm in the frosty air.

At midnight, another company, far more
silent and stealthy, wound its way up the hills,
and camped in the neck of the valley. Masoud
woke before dawn and started at the sight.
There was something strangely familiar in the
group of low-spreading black tents, recalling
the days of long ago when he had grown to
know them so well as the home of Khalil.
Masoud lost no time in saddling his horse, and
riding away in the opposite direction.

He made his way safely out of sight and
turned down a valley leading to another group

of mountains.   He had to dismount and lead his horse around a bad bit of rock.

"Thank God, that is over!" and he started to remount, when he was confronted by half a dozen horsemen.

"You are ours at last, you dog!" one cried; and they bound him hand and foot.

They took him to the tent of Khalil's father, and the sheikhs of the tribe were called to hold the trial.   Masoud stood silent, as the group assembled.

At last Khalil's father rose and chanted in impromptu meter the story of his three sons, his only children, lost in one day.   The old men responded with dreary wails; there was not a dry eye among them.

Masoud was placed in the midst and a circle drawn about him on the ground.   A rod was put into his hand and the formula repeated for him to swear:

> In the name of this rod,
> And Almighty God,
> And the seal that for Solomon, David's son, stood,
> I swear I am innocent of this blood.

Masoud began to speak the words, but his voice trembled.   He dropped the rod——

"I cannot swear; I am guilty."

He covered his face and a deep silence fell upon the company.

It was broken by the sobs of Khalil's father, sobs filled with the loneliness of years. His three sons were gone irrevocably. Should he add to their loss yet another life? He held out his hands, and spoke:

"Young man, I take you to be my son in the place of my three lost ones."

Masoud started and looked from one to another. The hard faces, steeled to bloodshed and death, were broken with weeping.

"My son, do you not believe me?" said the old man.

Masoud took the wrinkled, outstretched hand and bent his head reverently over it. One by one the elders stole away and the father and his strange son remained alone.

"I shall never leave you," breathed Masoud. And he kept his word. It became a proverb in the tribe:

"He loves as Masoud loves his father."

II

HONOR IN THE DESERT

MILHEM, Musbah, and Arif were hungry. Of course, they had no money and the few camels which they had owned, their only possession, had been killed by an unusual frost on the desert. They consulted together; there was but one thing to do; they would go out on a search for plunder, for "what Allah might send," they said.

They begged a little food from the sheikh and started out. It was a dreary tramp, nothing but yellow clay and a few thorn-patches to be seen. By the end of the first day, Milhem threw himself upon the ground. "It is better to rest," he said, "than to labor for that which comes not." So Musbah and Arif went

16

on another day alone. By this time their
food was exhausted and Musbah became discouraged. "You may go on by yourself," he
said.

Arif plodded on till the end of the third
day, when he came upon a drove of camels in a
sheltered valley; the keepers were asleep. In
the midst was a stuffed camel-calf, used to
keep the flock together. Arif cut the bands
by which the camels were hobbled, lifted the
stuffed camel-calf in his arms and started
away, the whole drove silently following.
When he was far enough off from the camp
to feel safe, he stopped to milk the camels and
refresh himself; then he traveled on, followed
by the herd, to the place where he had left
Musbah. His companion was greatly amazed
to see his booty.

"To Allah be the praise!" said Arif.

They journeyed on merrily together till
they found Milhem.

"Get up, son of a thousand sluggards! Are
you still sleeping, like yeast?" cried Musbah.
"See what Allah has sent us!"

The three returned to camp together. Then
came the quarrel,—Musbah and Milhem claim-

ing equal shares with Arif in the booty. Being unable to reach a decision, they went to the kadi, the judge.

He listened to them solemnly, then after a silence spoke: "You, Arif, the true plunderer, are entitled to the herd as your lawful capture. However, you shall allow Musbah, who went with you two days, to choose one camel for himself, and if he chooses the best one, it will be but according to agreement. You yourself shall choose a camel for Milhem, who went with you but one day, and if you choose the worst one, he will have nothing to answer. The rest of the herd is yours."

The three men started away satisfied.

The judge called them back. "Perhaps you would like to know whose the camels were before you captured them. They were *mine*. But Allah forbid that I should claim them back, when they have been captured according to the honorable laws of plunder. Allah grant you blessing in their possession!"

III

THE MOURNING FOR SIGR *

THE fame of Sigr, the Anezeh Hero, had spread among all the tribes of the desert. Bedouin maidens sang of him at their feasts, and his enemies fled at the mention of his name.

Sang the maidens:

Alone standeth Sigr, the Rock of the Anezeh,
In battle, in plunder, in honor, in craft;
The palm-branches envy the grace of his form,
The storm-clouds of heaven bend above him
To learn more of power and of majesty grand.

At the height of his glory, Sigr gathered his horsemen, his fifty undaunted ones, and they swept through the desert to the pasturing lands of their rivals, the great Beni Bekr.

* After the dithyrambs of the desert.

With level spears, they swooped upon the herdsmen, capturing from them what they counted their great glory, their flock of choice white camels.

Great was the fury of the Beni Bekr, who set forth two hundred strong to take revenge. They met in a narrow valley, two hundred opposed to fifty!

Then Sigr rode forth in the presence of all and cried boldly:

> I am Sigr the hero,
> The universe is my war-horse,
> The vault of heaven my saddle-bow.
> I challenge you, warriors of the Beni Bekr,
> Come fight me in single combat,
> I will feed to the vultures your carcasses,
> Your bones to the wolves of the desert!

The Beni Bekr reined in their horses, and stood looking from one to the other. Then came forth from among them Asad, son of Ali. and answered:

> I scorn your boasting, O Sigr,
> 'Tis the babble of an infant,
> The chirp of a locust;
> What is Sigr before Asad,
> The lion of the Beni Bekr!

The two bands of warriors pushed back on the opposite slopes of the valley and left the space open between for the champions. They took their places one at each end of the valley, then bending forward charged on one another with their javelins. The horses passed at a wild gallop and Asad of the Beni Bekr lay motionless upon the ground. In rage, another champion, Jabir, son of Amr, came down to avenge the wrong; but he, too, was laid low. Warrior followed warrior, none could hold out against Sigr the Hero. The Beni Bekr could bear it no longer; regardless of all rules of honor, they rushed down upon him and cut him to pieces.

The news of his death swept through the desert like the angry sirocco and from far and near came the mourners to mourn at his tent. They wept that he died in the height of his triumph, they wept that he died by the baseness of men of mean spirit, they wept that he died far away from his kindred, with none of his own blood to show him their last respect.

But while they lamented, the messenger sped on his journey, two days through the fiery desert, to Sigr's elder sister, Safah, wife of

Dib the Wolf. He found her, all unmindful, making butter in her goatskin churn.

"The Lord fulfil to you," he said, "the days of him who is departed."

Then Safah knew and loudly did she wail, rending her long flowing robe from top to hem and throwing dust upon her head.

The whole camp assembled and the messenger chanted the praises of Sigr the dead.

> I sing of Sigr, the pride of the Anezeh,
> The dawn arose only to publish his might.
> His brow was his bow and his glance the arrow
> That smote with dismay the heart of his foe.
> Seven pashas sat on the mat at his feet
> Waiting only to do his commands.
> Oh seek through the desert, the home of the Arabs;
> Not one will be found who is worthy to serve
> Pouring water upon Sigr's hands.

The messenger ceased, and the company broke into mad cries of grief and curses on all who ever had named the name of the Beni Bekr. Only one sat unmoved, Dib the Wolf. His wife stood before him, her eyes flashing fire.

"I must go and wail for my brother."

But what cared Dib the Wolf for Sigr, as

long as his own wants were met? He dismissed the assembly with cursing and wrath and called to his wife, "Bring me my argileh!"

The fire did not die from her eyes, but in silence she filled the argileh, placed upon it with her bare fingers a glowing coal from the hearth, and presented it meekly to her lord. Then she hasted and made coffee for him, and his spirit was soothed, and he slept.

Then Safah rose in haste, stealing her way between the kneeling camels of the camp, till she was in the open wilderness. She stayed not nor looked back till a day's journey lay behind her. Then she threw herself upon the ground to sleep. In two hours she rose again, and at the dawn of the second day she mourned with the women in the tent of Sigr.

But in the meantime another messenger sped on his way to the north, where the younger sister lived, Amneh, wife of Za'al of Aleppo. Five days he journeyed, till he found her at the tent of her lord. But Za'al had a spirit fiercer even than that of Dib the Wolf. Not for naught had his mother called him by the name of Za'al, Anger!

"Should I send my wife five days' journey to weep for an Anezeh hero?"

And the messenger fled, not daring to face his displeasure.

But when the night fell, and all the camp slept, Amneh arose. She took an earthenware bottle of water, a handful of dates in her girdle. With these she set forth for a five days' journey through the desert. By night her guides were the stars; by day, the bleached skeletons of the camels which lay with outstretched necks along the caravan route. Hurrying on through the starlight, she heard the laugh of the hyena, as he made his ungainly way toward her. He stopped to watch her from among his rocks and meditated running against her and throwing her down; for a hyena will not attack an enemy in upright position. But there was something dauntless in the bold figure of the woman braving her way alone through the night, and the hyena slunk away to seek his victims among the fallen along the caravan route.

She took her scanty sleep by day, when the sun burned most fiercely. The vulture spied her from his height and fancied her one of his victims; he screamed to his mates, and together they circled about her. They drew nearer and nearer, and their necks were craned for the final swoop downward, when she rose with a bound and bent forward again upon her hardy task.

Ten days had the mourners lamented for Sigr when the tent door was darkened by a bold, gaunt figure; it was Amneh, wife of Za'al of Aleppo. Together she and her sister Safah raised their arms to heaven, and beat their breasts for the fate of their brother.

Cried Amneh:

> Would that the heavens were my scroll,
> The cedar of Lebanon my pen,
> The vast ocean my ink-pot;
> Then would I write the deeds of Sigr,
> Sigr the rock, the hero.

And Safah answered:

> Tears have I wept for thee, O my brother,
> Till they roll like a flood about me.
> Let their billows flow over our souls,
> Let them bear us together afar,
> To the distant abode of Sigr our brother.

And thus was the mourning accomplished, the forty days' mourning for Sigr.

SPRINGS IN A DRY LAND

Syrian Woman

IV

FOR THE SAKE OF SHEFFAKA

THE head of Abu-Fahad was bent upon his breast as he rode. Not so was he accustomed to lead his Bedouin spearmen on their raids upon the hamlets of the plain. His blooded mare, with dainty fore feet, picked her way among the rolling stones, arching her neck to feel her master's guidance; but the silver-mounted reins fell limp upon her mane. The mind of Abu-Fahad still lingered at the village camping-ground which he had left; the open space was still before him, the ring of kneeling camels with heads turned to the center, the loosened burdens on the ground, the shifting group of Bedouin merchants, bartering, smoking, or spreading out their prayer-rugs to the south. And then appeared the Christian preacher, Murad of Lebanon, whose custom was to wander in and out among the tribes. Abu-Fahad had heard report about this youth with earnest face and winning speech, but he had never met him face to face before.

Murad's eye fell on the prayer-rugs, and he spoke respectfully: "Yes, truly God is greater; we should ever turn to him in prayer."

"His name be honored," answered Abu-Fahad. "It is he who giveth victory to the faithful and maketh them to glory over all their foes."

"Have you never known the greater glory?" asked Murad; "the glory and the beauty of Sheffaka, Compassion?" and opening his Book, he gave his message in eager and appealing words; man's need of mercy and his holy privilege to show compassion to his fellow man.

And now, while Abu-Fahad rode in silence, wrapt in thought, there grew within him a strange desire, unknown till now, for the angel presence, even in his own fierce heart, of Sheffaka, Compassion.

Thus musing, he overtook a wayfarer, plodding the stony road on foot.

"Rest be to you," he said.

"The Lord return you rest," answered the traveler, but as he spoke he tightened up his girdle, showing his dagger in its sheath.

"Have no fear," said Abu-Fahad, thinking how readily the day before he would have called upon a traveler to deliver up his money-girdle and his arms.

They traveled on in friendliness together for many hours. At last they came to a small rill trickling beneath a rock.

"Water is the gift of God," said the walker; "let us stop."

Abu-Fahad alighted from his horse, loosened the bridle to let the thirsty creature drink, and then the two men rested in the patch of shade, the spicy smell of mint and thyme adding its sweet refreshment.

"Bread also is the gift of God," said Abu-Fahad, and loosening his tasseled saddle-bags he divided with the stranger the food that he had brought for two days' journey.

"And now let us go on," said Abu-Fahad, "and seeing I have had my share of rest, I will

change places with you for a while, you riding
and I on foot."

"I beg forgiveness of the Lord," exclaimed
the stranger. "His curse would be on me for
taking such a privilege from one above me in
station and in years."

But Abu-Fahad pressed him and he yielded.

As one is carried on the light wings of a
dream, so the low-born stranger felt himself
borne forward by the fleet-footed creature of
the desert. As though he upheld the rainbow,
great was his exultation, and the mad purpose seized him to ride away forever and leave
his benefactor to his own folly in trusting to a
stranger.

A tightening of the rein was all-sufficient,
and the high-bred animal leaped forward.

"Hold!" cried the astonished owner.

But the new joy of gain was too alluring.

> Contented like the willow,
> Whose roots are in the water,

caroled the usurper with insulting triumph.

"Listen!" cried Abu-Fahad, with a tone of
just rebuke which forced obedience. "You
have my mare, I do not ask you to return her,

that is beyond my power. I have but one
request. For the sake of him who thus en-
riches you, grant it, I pray."

The stranger's shamed humanity could not
refuse. "I grant it."

"This is my request," said Abu-Fahad.
"Never, by the life which Allah gave you,
never tell how you obtained your mare."

"That is not likely," laughed the stranger,
trying to cover his confusion under a garb of
insolence. "But what reason have you for
such a strange request?"

Abu-Fahad answered gravely, "Because
then you would be a murderer."

"A murderer!" cried the stranger.

"Yes," repeated Abu-Fahad, "you would
kill Sheffaka, Compassion, in the hearts of
men. If it were told that Abu-Fahad was deceived, lending his mare in pity to a stranger,
then nevermore would any rider lend his mare
to help a traveler on."

The traitor, crushed with guilt, slipped from
the saddle, covering Abu-Fahad's hands and
feet with kisses. "Oh, let me kneel on burning
coals and beg God for the sake of Sheffaka to
forgive my sin."

Eagerly he forced Abu-Fahad back into the saddle, beseeching him to leave him in his shame.

And Abu-Fahad rode away, again absorbed in thought, but as he turned upon the rocky path, he raised his head for one last backward look toward the stranger, and there he saw him kneeling on the ground, his face bent low and buried in his hands.

V

THE MARK OF
THE CROSS

I

THE Bedouin encampment of Sheikh
Selim presented its usual noonday appearance of listlessness and neglect.
Most of the men were away with the herds,
and the few loungers left behind were smoking in silence or lying asleep in the sun. The
women were grouped together here and there,
making butter or rocking their babies, both by
the same contrivance, a goatskin hung between
three poles and shaken violently back and
forth.

Among the groups trudged a forlorn little
figure carrying bundles of brushwood to the
various tents. No one noticed her large-eyed,

wistful face. Plainly the child was by long
usage the little camp drudge.

After finishing her task without appearing
to seek or expect commendation, she slung
some goatskin water-bottles over the back of a
tiny donkey and drove him from the camp.
She found it discouraging work getting him
past alluring clumps of dry thistles, which he
tackled with a determination worthy of a better feast, nibbling down the sharp points before attempting the tough spiny whole. Little Najla belabored him lustily, with many
imprecations upon his kind, and she was panting for breath when she brought him at last
to a sluggish rill on the edge of the desert.

The footprints of many animals had turned
the muddy water-bed into a sort of morass,
and into this ooze she drove her donkey, following him with her bare feet. With the un-
concern of long habit she filled the bottles with
the muddy water which the animals had stirred
up, and started the donkey up the bank by a
loud "Hanghk!"

But here her energy seemed to leave her and
she gave way to the melancholy which had become her deepest feeling. She crouched upon

the bank, her chin upon her knees, staring va-
cantly into the slimy water.

"O Allah! why have you cursed me?"

She drew back the loose drapery of her
sleeve and moodily studied the tattooing on her
arm. It was the usual indigo stain that the
Bedouins employ, but the figures were strange,
to Najla without meaning; only one stood out
distinctly, large and dark and seeming to over-
shadow all the others, the figure of a cross.

She wet her left hand in the water and mechanically rubbed the markings.

"If they would only wash out, I might be
free from the curse." She held her arm out
at full length. "There is nothing beautiful
in it; if it were only marked like the arm of
the sheikh's daughter, with seven spreading
palm-trees!"

Najla was suddenly startled by a rustling in
the scraggy bushes at her side. She looked
up into a face that frightened her with its wild
eagerness.

"Where did you get those marks?" asked the
stranger hoarsely.

Najla pulled down her sleeve in shame, too
confused to answer.

"Is your name Najla?" asked the young man again.

"How did you know?" exclaimed Najla in large-eyed wonder.

"Look here!" he cried, and pulling up his own sleeve, he revealed to Najla's astonished gaze an arm marked with the same figures as hers.

"Don't you remember your brother Faris?" he asked. "Think, when you were a little, little girl!"

"When my mother was alive? Yes, I had forgotten all about it; he used to carry me on his back."

"Yes, and you used to run about with silver anklets on your feet, with bells on them, and they tinkled wherever you went. Does this help you to remember?" and Faris pulled out from his bosom a child's anklet such as he had described.

Najla grasped it. "Oh how wonderful! I remember it perfectly, and they took the other away from me and beat me for losing this."

"Poor little Najla!" said Faris, taking both her hands, "how cruel it was for me to run away from you after our parents died; but I meant even then in my folly to come back for you sometime, and I took the anklet away to prove that you belonged to me."

"Where did you go?" asked Najla.

"It's a wonder that I ever got anywhere," said Faris, "you know I was only eight years old. I wandered about almost perishing for food and water. One time, I came upon a wolf-trail, seven parallel tracks; you know the creatures travel abreast, because if one of them should fall, those behind would spring upon him and devour him."

"Horrible!" exclaimed Najla. "What if they found you!"

"They would have found me that night," said Faris, "but I was picked up by some cameleers, who took me a long journey to a town. They left me in a mission school kept by a foreigner. The gentleman was a doctor and people came to him from all the country round to be cured. At first I said to myself, 'What a wicked man he must have been that he needs now to earn all this merit to atone for his past!' But I learned afterward how mistaken I was. Do you know why he did it?"

Faris again eagerly caught his sister's hand. "It was because of the story on your arm!"

Najla looked aghast with amazement. "You are mad, my brother; what do you mean?"

"Oh, it's a beautiful story," Faris continued. "My teacher's wife used to seat me on a little chair beside her and lay her soft hand on my arm, pointing out the different figures and telling me about them."

"What! have these marks a meaning?" exclaimed Najla.

"Look!" said Faris, holding her wrist. "This cross is the center of all, and the long figure beside it is a ladder, and here is a hammer, with three nails, and a sponge on the end of a staff, and this above is a crown;—oh, Najla, it was a crown of thorns."

"I don't understand," said Najla.

"Of course not, poor little sister," said Faris, "but I will tell you about it, over and over, till you love it better than anything else in the world. Don't you remember when our mother used to tell it?"

"No," said Najla. "Did she know it?"

"Why, Najla," said Faris, "our mother was

a Christian girl and our father carried her away from her village home and made her his wife; you can't remember how she used to weep for her own people. She would talk to me about it, small as I was. She was so afraid that we children would grow up without knowing about the cross that she tattooed the story upon our arms, believing that sometime some one would tell us what it meant."

"But a Christian is a base, mean thing," said Najla, still perplexed. "I suppose that is why the tribe all curse me."

"Little sister," said Faris, "I am going to take you away from all that, away over the Black River to the land of the Christians."

"The Black River!" gasped Najla. "The jinn would catch us!"

"What are you talking about?" asked Faris.

Najla lowered her voice, her black eyes dilated with horror. "Don't you know how Suleiman, the father of our tribe, went to a wise woman to find a cure for the illness of his wife? And she gave him a drink that showed him his wife's heart, and there he saw a horrible jinn crouched upon it pressing out the life! Then, by the power that the wise woman gave him, he exorcised the demon and banished him into the Black River, where he is imprisoned to this day, waiting for any member of our tribe to cross the stream, that he may catch him and devour him!"

Faris laughed gaily. "Najla, there are no such things as jinn. Look at me! I have crossed that river twice!"

Najla gazed at him stupefied. "Perhaps you have a charm."

A sudden bright smile lighted Faris' face.

"Yes, I have, it is a beautiful promise that God has sent us. He says, 'when thou passest through the waters, I will be with thee'."

Najla was incredulous. "Allah rules the Adamies,* but will the jinn obey him? No, by the sheikh's tent pole, I cannot go."

Faris looked at her in perplexity. "How shall I make you understand? Won't you believe it? You are God's child; you have his marks upon your arm; no jinn, if there were such things, would have power over you."

Najla's eyes blazed with a new light. "Do you mean that when the jinn saw the holy marks on my arm, he would be afraid?"

* Children of Adam.

"Yes," said Faris gently, "if you wish to think of it that way; you will understand better by and by."

Najla clasped her hands, her lips quivered and the eyes that she raised to Faris' face were glistening with mingled fear and trust. "My brother, I will go with you, if it is to life or death."

Faris took her hands in his. "Let us go at once; my horse is here and we can gallop away before any one sees us."

Najla's serious face broke into a smile of amused compassion. "How innocent you are! We might as well hang to the ropes of the wind! The Bedouins would track us before we had found our road."

"Then what can we do?" asked Faris.

Najla thought a while. "In the first place, we must give no suspicion that I am with you, and then we must let them hunt a while before there is any chance of finding us."

"It seems to me you are requiring impossibilities," said Faris.

"Oh, no!" said Najla, warming with her plan. "You might go as a guest to the Suleib camp over beyond those knolls four hours away. I shall return to our camp;—and a glorious greeting they will give me too, after all this delay! In the night, I shall steal away over the rocks; they show no footprints! I know of an ancient cistern over there, an hour away, where I can hide for three days, while the tribe tire themselves out hunting the high-roads. By that time, they will think I have been eaten by wolves and will give up the search. It will then be safe for you to meet me with your horse."

"You could beat the Sheitan!" exclaimed Faris admiringly. Then a new thought struck him. "What will you do for food those three days?"

"I can live on very little," she answered meaningly. "We Bedouins keep alive because even death is so scarce!"

They kissed each other solemnly and parted. "For three days or forever!" said Faris.

II

Najla drove her donkey into camp under a fire of imprecations.

"Your life be cut off!"

"Your light be put out!"

And as a climax, "Allah send you a husband to beat you twice a day!"

But she went on with her work apparently
indifferent, and in the night fled with swift
and noiseless footsteps over the rocks.

The ancient rain-water cistern which she had
chosen made a good hiding-place, its narrow
mouth being overgrown with bushes, which
quite concealed the large pear-shaped chamber
below. Najla pulled aside a bush and peered
down into the inky blackness, shuddering,
knowing that she could never climb out of such
a place alone. It took all her courage to let
herself down over the edge. She dropped
upon the dry stony bottom unhurt, but shiver-
ing with terror. The darkness seemed to close
in upon her, unbroken save by the glimmer of
a few stars shining through the bushes overhead. She cowered upon the floor where she
had dropped, not daring to touch the unseen
walls of the place, which her overwrought mind
filled with venomous creatures. Alone! alone!
The great world stretching above her was now
hopelessly out of reach. What if Faris should
never come!

Daylight came at last as an intense relief,

showing the cistern walls to be but harmless rock and old plaster, and she was glad now to lean against them, to avoid being seen from above. All day her ears were straining for the sound of footsteps, but only the silence answered her. She used her scant supply of food and the water in her small earthen bottle as frugally as possible, but the time was long and soon there was nothing left but frantic thirst and feverish visions of Bedouins pursuing from behind and jinn starting up in the river before her.

In the meantime Faris had made his way toward the Suleib camp. As he approached it, he was overtaken by a man riding a large white ass, and Faris saw by the gazelle-skin tunic which he wore that he was one of the Suleibs.

"I am your *dakhil,* your suppliant," Faris said.

"The dakhil is sent by God," answered the Suleib, "come with me to the camp."

Faris obeyed gladly, but with difficulty kept his horse up with the rapid pace of the ass. His companion looked back at him with a complacent smile.

"When the other tribes degraded us from using horses," he said, "they did not foresee that we should outstrip them with our humble asses, but so it was decreed."

They were now at the camp, a forlorn group of goatskin shelters, hardly to be dignified as tents. Faris knew that the Suleibs were the poorest of all the tribes, but for that reason at war with none, and so the more likely to protect him.

He was met with kindness and taken to a tent, where the supper of dried gazelle-meat was placed before him.

"We serve you with the food of our people," said the sheikh. "Our hunters, with their gazelle-skin robes, can track down the herds without frightening them. Allah, who has deprived us of flocks, has thus given us a recompense."

"His name be exalted," said Faris.

"Pardon me," said the sheikh, as Faris reached out his hand. "Is that a charm branded on your wrist?"

Faris flushed, he had not meant thus to reveal himself. "My secrets are in your hands," he said.

"And will they not be held sacred?" answered the sheikh with wrath. "*W'Allah!* let
the Arabs despise us as they may, never would
a Suleib reveal the secrets of his dakhil."

"Then I will tell you about it," said Faris.
"It belongs to you as much as to me."

The dusky group listened in rapt attention
while Faris told them the story of the cross.

"That sounds to me," said one, who had seen
something of the towns, "like the cursed religion of the Nazarenes."

"Call no man's religion cursed," said Faris,
"until you know all about it; and least of all
curse the Holy One who died upon the cross;
such curses only return upon him who utters
them."

"The lad is right," said the sheikh. "None
but a holy man would have given himself for
others."

As Faris was leaving the tent, a young man
plucked him by the sleeve. "Tell me more,"
he said, "about that wonderful story. Do you
know," he added lowering his voice, "that
some say our Suleib tribe was originally
Christian, that they were named for the cross,
the *salib;* and in olden times the men of our

tribe all had on their shoulders the same mark
of the cross that you have on your arm."

Before sunrise the next morning, Faris
heard angry voices outside his tent.

"You are sheltering a vagabond townsman,
a low, contemptible beast, a tiller of the
ground. Fry his heart in his blood!"

"But what proof have you that he stole the
girl?" asked Faris' host.

"Proof enough!" with an oath. "We found
her cursed footsteps on the bank, some above
and some below his, showing they were there
together. We know that he is a townsman by
the fashion of his shoes, and young, by the
firmness of his tread; and that he came to you,
his horse's footprints testify all the way. The
inference is clear, he has brought her here
to you!"

"At what hour did you say the girl disappeared?" asked the Suleib sheikh.

"She was with us till midnight," was the
answer. "She must have escaped before
dawn."

The Suleib sheikh answered exultantly, "I
can prove to you that our guest arrived here
at sunset, hours before the girl escaped, her

flight has nothing to do with him. Come this way and look at his horse and tell me if he has just come in from a four hours' journey? Feel his muscles, you can see that he has rested all night; look at the mud on his feet, that is not fresh mud! And now come look at the hoof-prints; they are already blown over with dust, surely no man with the keenness of the Bedouin could say those marks were less than twelve hours old!"

The Bedouin examined the marks carefully, biting his lips with annoyance, then bent down and smelled the hoof-print. "Yes, the odor is gone," he said. "The truth is with you."

He left disappointed, and Faris was undisturbed for the remainder of his time.

On the third day he said good-by to the Suleibs and started off in the opposite direction from his destination. When he was well out of sight, he took a roundabout track and reached the old cistern by nightfall. No one was visible. He eagerly pulled aside the bushes and called down.

"Najla, little sister, are you there?"

"Faris!" answered a weak choking voice from the darkness.

Faris quickly unwound his girdle, and, letting down one end, gently drew Najla up.
The exhausted child threw herself upon his
neck in tears. He soothed her with awkward
tenderness.

"Drink this leben," * he said, holding a small
leather bottle to her lips. "There! You can
do anything now!"

He swung her up on the saddle behind him
and they were off at last.

The journey was one of many days in a
burning wilderness, often without food or
water. What saved them more than once
was Najla's surreptitious milking of the
goats!

At last Faris pointed out a line of green in
the distance. "There is the Black River!"

Najla grasped his arm tightly; "But the
jinn is there! Oh brother, I cannot cross!"

Just then a gun-shot sounded behind them.
They looked back in terror and saw the
Bedouins in hot pursuit.

"They have tracked us!" gasped Najla.

"God must decide it!" breathed Faris, bend-
* Milk artificially soured; a common article of diet
with the Arabs.

ing forward and putting his spurs into his horse.

The creature bounded ahead to the utmost of his jaded strength, while the shots continued from behind. The two were now close upon the stream. Najla, doubly terrified, clung to her brother.

"Remember you are God's child," he said.

She buried her face upon her brother's shoulder and lifted her bare right arm, with the cross upon it, above her head, while the horse dashed through the shallow stream and struggled up the opposite bank.

"We are safe!" cried Faris.

They hurried up the farther bank as the baffled pursuers reached the stream and stopped.

"They will not follow us," cried Najla. "They have no cross to protect them."

The Bedouins turned back in rage, and Faris and Najla rode on to the new life.

VI

BESHARA, THE BEARER OF TIDINGS

I

A RIDER picked his way along the edge of the Syrian desert. An anachronism he might have seemed, a son of the East and the West alike, his matter-of-fact European dress relieved by the white traveling robe over his shoulders, and the lingering touch of Orientalism, the red fez, which served well to set off his handsome dark features and thoughtful brow.

Beshara's mind surged back over a multitude of far-away recollections as he rode. Could it be that he was the same eager student who went to Beirut to college? The memory made him heart-sick.

Only a year before he had grasped in triumph his medical diploma, and had gone forth to be a man of power in his country. He had settled in a seaport city, where foreign customs were growing. "There will be a demand for doctors there," he thought. But so, alas! thought others of his kind, and as the year wore by Beshara in bitterness found himself without employment.

Now in desperation he must return to his far-away inland home.

He rode on gloomily, absent-mindedly. Suddenly his mind-picture shifted. He looked about with startled alertness, the rocks, the undulations of the plain, were new to him; he had lost his way. He sought to retrace his steps, but to no avail. As time wore on, his horse went lame; Beshara dismounted to lead him—whither? With eager eye he detected some dark objects in the distance. He made his way painfully toward them over the rolling stones of a dried water-course; his horse gasped with every breath, and with pleading human eyes seemed to beg for a chance to lie down and die.

Man and beast revived as they drew nearer

and made out the low black tents of a Bedouin encampment. They were greeted from afar by an onset of barking from the camp-dogs and hooting from the half-clothed barbarian children. These were silenced by a young man in dirty flowing robes who came forward with a salute of welcome: *"Marhaba!* (Greetings!)"

"Marhabtein! (Double greetings!)," answered Beshara.

"Welcome! Most welcome!" said the youth. "Come, prefer yourself at the tent of the sheikh."

"The preference is from you," answered Beshara. "But, my horse, can anything be done for him?"

"Come this way to Abu Sharr. There is no skill like his in all the world!"

"Abu Sharr! 'Father of Evil'! What a name!" thought Beshara, but in politeness said nothing.

They were now the center of a curious and vivacious group, each clamoring with his own advice.

"Cursed be the father of children!" cried the guide, cuffing the heads of the younger marauders, and opening a way through the group of men to greet the esteemed Abu Sharr.

The case was explained and the horse examined. Abu Sharr stroked his chin solemnly.

"You have your choice of three remedies. You can bleed the horse, put in a seton, or pierce his nostril."

"Is there nothing else?" asked Beshara, his surgical and medical training rising in double protest.

Abu Sharr gave a withering glance. "I raised horses before you were strapped into your cradle."

Beshara was tossed helplessly between the horns of the dilemma.

"I am under your orders," he said. "As you tell me to choose, let us try bleeding—though the poor creature has little blood to spare!" he added under his breath.

Abu Sharr with a deft motion pricked the two front veins in the horse's knees; then, to Beshara's dismay, mounted and started off at a jog-trot, leaving a double red track on the clay behind him.

"Stop!" cried Beshara, "the horse is already exhausted; he is sick from overwork!"

But by this time Abu Sharr was beyond call.
The horse at first could hardly take a step
without stumbling, but to Beshara's amazement, as the rider urged him on, his step became visibly firmer. At the end of a half-
hour, he returned on a canter, head erect, his
eyes clear, and his whole bearing improved.

"He will be good for a journey to-morrow,"
said Abu Sharr, dismounting.

Beshara was now taken to the tent of the
sheikh and received with the hospitality which
is the Arab's glory. He was given the seat of
honor, while the elders ranged themselves in a
solemn circle about him. Pipes were served
and smoked in silence. Only at intervals did
the sheikh break the spell by some question
about the journey or some renewed expression
of welcome. In the center of the group the
sheikh's son pounded coffee in a carved wooden
mortar, beating out with the pestle a sort of
rhythmic tune. The coffee was then prepared
over a brazier and poured out, frothy and
sugarless, into tiny cups.

The supper came later. A copper pot was
lined with dates, the gigantic pie thus formed
being filled with melted butter and placed,

steaming hot, in the center of the group. The guests tore off morsels of their tough bread and dipped them into the common dish. They drank from earthenware jugs which they held high above their heads, while the water poured from the nozzle in a long stream into the drinker's throat. Two men stood throughout the meal, holding aloft lighted lanterns. The meal was concluded in silence. Then Beshara rose and saluted the sheikh. *"Deimi!* (Forever!)" he said, leaving it to the company to interpret, "May God establish forever your hospitable board."

"May God establish forever your life," answered the sheikh. "You have eaten bread and salt with us now; henceforth we are brothers."

The dining-room was easily converted into a bedroom, the guests rolling themselves in their rugs and sleeping upon the ground.

Beshara awoke refreshed, and found, contrary to all his former knowledge of cause and effect, maladies and their cures, that his horse was now in excellent condition for the day's journey.

The sheikh walked with him toward the open space where the horses were picketed.

Beshara's foot was in the stirrup when a pleading voice caught his ear. He turned and saw a woman with a baby on her back.

"May Allah preserve those beautiful black eyes! Tell me truly did you come from the great school for doctors at Beirut?"

"Yes, truly," answered Beshara, smiling.

"Allah lengthen your life! Look at my child! See this great swelling on his neck; he can neither eat nor sleep."

Beshara's heart had always warmed toward little children since the days in the Johanniter Hospital, when he used to carry them upstairs in his arms. He examined the baby and relieved it at once.

"Mashallah!" exclaimed the sheikh, "we did not know that one was with us with power from God. I beseech you come and see a poor fellow in this tent who was shot in the side."

Beshara followed the sheikh into a dark hole, a reveling place for microbes. He kneeled down beside the patient.

"The ball is here," he said, placing his finger six inches from the wound.

"Allah has revealed it to you!" exclaimed the sheikh, dumbfounded.

"I cannot take it out," said Beshara, "as I have neither dressings nor drugs."

"We will send for everything," said the sheikh, "only stay."

Beshara considered. "There are many difficulties; I should have to change the whole treatment. What has been done so far?" and he noticed more closely the worn face of the patient.

"They cup and bleed me," groaned the sufferer, "to keep down the fever."

Beshara repressed a smile as he recognized the skill of Abu Sharr.

The sheikh's eyes almost twinkled. "We know how to raise horses here," he said, "but who can tell what is concealed within the body of a son of Adam?"

"But those who have treated the patient will not want to give up to me——"

"When the Sheikh Mustafa says a thing," answered the host, "it is so."

He drew Beshara out of the tent.

"Hurry up there!" he called.

A man appeared, leading a dainty creature, graceful, light, sensitive, one of the world-famed mares of the desert.

"Ruaib is her name," said the sheikh to Beshara. "She is yours."

And thus it was that Beshara was installed as surgeon-general in the camp of Sheikh Mustafa.

II

Beshara threw himself eagerly into his new work. His heart and bright young face aglow with zeal, he served the tribe with the intelligence, the skill, the science, that had been given him.

He spent two hours making perfect his first antiseptic dressing. He left the tent to see another patient and returned in half an hour. The man, with grimy hands, had pulled the dressing off.

"Why did you do this?" asked Beshara.

"It was uncomfortable," answered the patient.

Beshara learned soon to expect such things as a matter of course.

He was no longer the guest of the tribe.

"Rather their slave," he said to himself. The coarseness, the uncleanliness of their gipsy life disgusted him, but he kept bravely on.

As time passed he noticed a strange unrest in the camp. Firearms were taken out and burnished; bags of dates and water-skins were collected. The conversation round the pipes was all of war and plunder.

"I remember," said Abu Sharr to the company, "how Asaad Nimr tried years ago to plunder in the name of our sheikh. His cursed features were something like those of Sheikh Mustafa, so he rode down upon an enemy calling out, 'I, Sheikh Mustafa, demand your surrender.' The coward was alarmed, and gave up at once his horse and arms and all he had. For a year Asaad boasted, till some one learned how he had taken his booty. The council was assembled, and without a dissenting voice it was voted that the plunder belonged to him whose name won it."

"Long live Sheikh Mustafa!" answered the men.

"Listen, my children," said the sheikh. "The raid must be by the way of the desert." He turned to Beshara.

"You will be ready to start with us at dawn. Take your bandages and medicines. This is what we have needed you for all this time."

Beshara leaped to his feet with flashing eyes. "Is this what you have tricked me into? to make me a highway robber? Take back your blooded mare; I leave you to-night!"

"Curse the religion of the Nazarenes!" cried the sheikh. "You will go with us if we carry your dead body." A dozen men grasped their knives as though to make good the threat.

"You would better not be a fool," said the sheikh.

"Truly," answered Beshara. He resumed his seat in silence, but his mind worked more fiercely than in his hardest student days.

They started at dawn. A few camels were taken to carry provisions and horse-feed. "And to bring back the booty," said Abu Sharr.

The warriors rode on horseback.

"We need not carry much water from here," said the sheikh. "We reach the well of the Eagle to-night, and will fill the water-skins for the two remaining days in the desert."

It was a burning ride through the sun-glare. During the noon rest, Beshara tested the temperature in the shadow of a kneeling camel— 105 degrees!

They plodded on, hour after hour, till the landscape swam and Beshara fancied himself forever moving on through a white waste of clay and stones. Only one thought remained clear before him—the well at sundown!

They reached it at last. The thirsty animals spied the clump of verdure from afar, and quickened their steps. Beshara leaped from his horse and threw himself full length upon the ground, to peer over the rocky brim into the water. A fetid odor rose up into his face. With dumb despair he saw the surface covered with floating dead locusts; on one side, half in the water, lay a dead wolf. Two days in the wilderness before them! A sudden hope rose in Beshara's breast: "They will have to turn back!"

He watched the sheikh's face. The grave countenance was as unmoved as when he was smoking his argileh in his own tent.

"My children," he said, "Bedouins never despair. We must sleep here to-night, and to-morrow take the two days' journey in one."

Without a murmur the men threw them-

selves upon the ground.   It was still like the
floor of an oven.

Before light they were roused.

"We have a little leben," said the sheikh, "to
divide among us this morning; we must keep
our last bag of pure water for noon."

The horses were quickly saddled. The poor
brutes, with parched tongues hanging out,
looked dumbly at the green water but would
not touch it.

The day's ride was past description—a day
when the fever burns and mounts into the brain
and men move in a horrible trance. The sirocco wind, robbed by the desert of every drop
of moisture, wrapped itself round them
as though to suck their life-blood. Columns
of dust stalked down upon them like genii
risen from some enchanter's bottle.

At noon they stopped for breath. Each man
was given two or three dates, and the precious
water-skin was unstrapped.

"The pebble, where is it?"

Abu Sharr produced it. Each man in turn
held it in the palm of his hand, and enough
water was poured into the palm to cover the
pebble. The last drops were poured out for

Sheikh Mustafa. "Allah Karim! God is gracious!" murmured the men.

They plodded on till sundown, when the sheikh called a halt of two hours. They loosened the horses' trappings and lay down in the open desert. The empty water-skins lay shriveled and cracked upon the ground beside them. The moon rose clear and full.

"Now for the last march!" cried the sheikh, "before you are water and life!"

The camels rose first, with awkward, plunging motion, and led the way; the horsemen followed, a phantom procession. They rode hour after hour in weary silence. The moon waned, till Beshara could discern nothing but the dim outline of the white camel before him, moving ever onward with monotonous swaying gait. He struggled with sleep as with some bird of evil omen that kept ever settling back upon him when he drove it off. At last the conflict grew too painful; he slipped down from his saddle, and in an instant was asleep upon the ground. Abu Sharr's horse stumbled over him.

"What in the name of madness are you doing?" exclaimed the rider.

"Leave me!" pleaded Beshara, "my life is nothing to me."

With rough kindliness the Bedouin jumped from his horse and forced Beshara back into his saddle.

"My son, you are not used to this life; we have only four hours more."

Four hours of suffering for man and beast! At last came the dawn, stretching ghostlike fingers across the plain; a mountain ridge took shape against the sky.

"Praise be to Allah! there is our well!" cried the sheikh. "Do you see the women with their water-skins?"

Water! water! who knows the life-giving meaning of the word! The men broke into cheers. The women, with eager sympathy, drew for them and their animals, and they drank with the gratitude of those who enter paradise.

When all were refreshed, the women filled their water-skins, slung them over the backs of their little donkeys, and trudged off to the Bedouin settlement at the base of the mountain. The sheikh waited till they were out of hearing, then rallied his men.

"The first village that we seek is up yonder at the head of the valley. We must sleep here at the well for the day; when night comes, we shall leave the camels here, and the horsemen will make the attack; with the help of Allah, we shall not leave so much as an onion-skin in the village!"

The men stretched themselves upon the ground. Beshara was the most exhausted of them all, but with a superhuman effort he kept himself awake.

"This is my high calling!" he kept saying to himself. In a short time all around him were deep in sleep. Without a sound he rose to his feet and hastened in the direction which the sheikh had pointed out. It was an hour's climb, a terrible task, but he panted on. The group of flat-roofed houses was reached. He hurried to the market-place, where the men were assembled.

"For your lives, defend yourselves! the Bedouins are upon you!"

From mouth to mouth the message flew, the whole village was astir. Men rushed hither and thither carrying arms and making barricades. Beshara, the bearer of the tidings, was

soon forgotten; he slipped behind a low arch,
his work now done, and threw himself upon
the ground and slept.

III

He was awakened at dark by the sound of
guns and conflict. He jumped up, all his
young blood on fire; then checked himself.
With hands clenched and lips pressed tightly
together, he struggled with himself. Should
he, Beshara, stand still while men defended
their homes? And yet, and yet, how could he
in honor fight? "I have eaten bread and salt
with them!" He stood, not caring that the
fighting came nearer. Torches gleamed,
weapons glanced back and forth. A sudden
weakness came over him; he was shot in the
arm. Like one in a dream he tried to stanch
the blood, but he was rapidly growing dizzy.

He was called to consciousness by a light
touch; the slight figure of a girl stood before
him.

"Come this way, quickly," she said, "there
is no time to lose."

He followed her, dazed, through rough al-
leys, up and down slippery steps, between

rows of huts. Smoke poured out of half-underground doorways from household fires upon the floor beneath, and in the fitful glare he could see huddled groups of women and children.

His guide led him to the outskirts of the village. "Take care," she said, "these steps are steep."

She seemed to disappear into the ground before him, but presently emerged, carrying a smoking clay lamp. He followed her down the steps, and found himself in a cave, roughly fitted up as a human habitation. An old woman came forward to greet him.

"Grandmother," said the girl, "this is the messenger who brought the warning."

"Welcome, oh, welcome he is among us!" she cried with quavering voice.

Beshara sank down upon a straw cushion on the floor.

"Grandmother," said the girl, "he is wounded; he has lost much blood."

As she spoke she brought from a corner a piece of soft material and tore it into strips.

"Let me wash the wound first," she said, bringing a jug of water.

With deft fingers, she started to bandage the arm.

"This way, please," said Beshara.

She grasped his meaning intelligently, and under his direction made a creditable dressing.

"Yasmin was always quick with her fingers," said the grandmother.

Yasmin! Jessamine! The name carried its own fragrance.

A halting step was heard on the stairway.

"Grandfather, is it you?"

"Yes, I come with joy; the Bedouins are driven away!"

"Praise the Lord!" cried they all.

The old man started at the sight of Beshara.

"You are the one I have sought all day! The whole village is calling for you; they are ready to kiss your feet!"

"Then they do not think me a coward?"

The old man looked perplexed. "What do you mean? They think you a prophet, a messenger from God." He caught sight of Beshara's bandaged arm. "And wounded, too! Truly we owe you our lives."

The old woman leaned forward. "My son, you have not told us your name."

"Beshara," he answered.

"Beshara!" she repeated, throwing up her hands in ecstasy, "and truly did your mother name you! 'The Bearer of Good Tidings!' Well is that name fulfilled to-night!"

The next morning the whole village crowded to do Beshara honor. They came with singing, dancing the sword-dance before him; never did a king receive more loyal tribute. They told him the story of the encounter and of the brave men who were wounded.

"Bring them to me," said Beshara. "I can use my right hand still; perhaps I can help them."

Their enthusiasm now knew no bounds.

"A great hakim is among us! With life and death in his hands!"

Beshara tended the wounded while the fever was still upon him, and the people who gathered around gazed as though upon a miracle.

"Oh, stay with us always!" they cried. "Men will come to you from all the villages round about; all eyes will look to you, the great hakim!"

The thought worked in Beshara's mind as he lay upon his pallet.

"I should not grow rich," he thought; his glance full upon the unselfish face of the girl, and his thought slank away for very shame.

"Tell me," said Yasmin eagerly, "did you truly come from the great college for doctors in Beirut?"

"Yes," said Beshara, "and, if I guess rightly, you, too, have not always been in this village."

Yasmin flushed, as she answered in English: "I was in the school of the English ladies in Nazareth."

"Oh, the noble English language!" exclaimed Beshara. "I have not heard it since I left the coast."

Yasmin brought out from her corner a pile of English books.

"It means to me all that is sweetest and best in my life," she said.

"What is that strange language that you are talking?" asked the grandmother.

"It is what they teach us in the schools," said Yasmin. From that time Beshara's love for the English language grew mightily.

"How can you be so happy," he asked Yasmin one day, "in such different surroundings from those where you have been educated?"

"I chose to come," she said. "I could not leave my grandparents alone. We used to have a house," she added apologetically, "but when my grandfather grew too old for work, we came here."

"What do you do when it rains? Does not the water pour down the steps?"

"Oh, we have dug a trench around inside the wall of the cave, so the water does not reach us," she said.

Beshara looked at her with a sort of awe.

IV

Several years later there arose on the bluff overlooking the village the cheerful red roof of the hakim's new house, the red-tiled roof, herald of the new civilization.

But the hakim himself had learned that a doctor's house in a country village is only a place to start from. He was again on horseback. He looked up lovingly to the archway, where stood Yasmin among her carnations and aromatic plants.

"Good-by, little wife," he called.

"Come back soon," she pleaded. "I tremble when you go to these distant villages."

"A hakim leads a charmed life," he cried; "never fear!" He turned down the steep path. How differently he had once panted up that way! Stopping at the last turn in the road, he waved his good-by once more to Yasmin, who still stood in the archway.

He had not told her that his road must again skirt the desert. He passed the well which he had journeyed so far to find, and rode on several hours upon the caravan path. No living thing did he see save a bright-eyed lizard that darted out from under a thorn-bush, and sat with arms akimbo watching the stranger.

He rode over a little eminence, and started at sight of a party of Bedouins just ahead of him, riding in the same direction as himself. With the alertness which the desert traveler learns, he stopped and waited till they should reach a safe distance. He watched them as they filed down a depression of the road between the rocks. Suddenly a demon yell burst forth, and like an avalanche there crashed down upon the party a band of armed men; the line was thrown back upon itself. They gathered themselves together, and struck forward again like a serpent, again and again, blow and repulse. But the attacking party had the advantage.

It seemed only a few minutes before Beshara saw the plunderers tie together the horses which remained unhurt, gather the weapons of their captives and gallop off. It was an episode which may occur any time on the desert.

A forlorn enough remnant was left, several figures lying motionless upon the ground, the rest bending over them.

Beshara could no longer stand by, an idle spectator. He made his way toward them; dismounting and leading his horse, he approached them on foot.

"I wish you peace."

He was answered by a groan from a wounded man in the center of the group.

"Give me space," said Beshara. "I think I can help him."

He bent down and started as from a blow. Yes, it was no other than Sheikh Mustafa! He glanced to the face opposite him, and met the sinister features of Abu Sharr!

"In the name of the Sheitan!" exclaimed Abu Sharr, clutching for his dagger; but the dagger had been carried away.

"Curse the religion of the beard——"

"Let us forget the past," said the sheikh. "My son, can you still have pity on an old man?"

Beshara lifted the sheikh's hand to his lips, then to his forehead.

"My father, I owe you my life; have I not eaten bread and salt with you?"

Carefully, tenderly, Beshara bound up the wounds. They improvised a stretcher out of their full girdles.

"We must carry him three hours to the nearest village," said Beshara.

After an hour's weary march, the sheikh stopped them. "Let me die here in peace."

They laid him upon the burning clay and tried to shield him from the sun with their bodies.

Suddenly the sheikh lifted himself up and spoke to Beshara.

"My son, when first you escaped from me, I

swore I would take your life; but now I know that God was with you."

He fell back heavily; Beshara caught him with his arm and laid him back upon the clay, lifeless.

GLANCES THROUGH THE LATTICE

Mohammedan Home

VII

HAJJEH FATMEH THE WISE

MANY years ago there lived a man of wealth and piety named Ahmed, who was inspired from above to make a pilgrimage to Mecca. Having no one to whom he could leave the care of his property during his absence, he sold all that he had and packed the money proceeds into an iron pail. He then sought for one whose wealth and rank should be so far raised above the sordid temptations of the more humble sons of Adam as to render him a safe custodian of his treasure. His thoughts turned to the kadi, or judge, the greatest man in his town. "Who," thought Ahmed, "is more worthy than he?" So to the kadi he went and committed his store, and then started forth upon his pilgrimage

In course of time he returned and hastened to pay his reverence to the great man
of the town. With the meek consciousness of
having obeyed heaven's precepts first, he asked
for his pail.

"Your pail!" exclaimed the kadi. "I know
of no pail. Guards, you have brought a mad-
man into my presence; turn him out!" And
the pious Ahmed found himself chased igno-
miniously from the court.

In his despair he sought counsel of Hajjeh
Fatmeh, a woman gifted with prudence and
discretion far beyond her sex.

She listened to his story with calm assurance. "Never fear," she said. "Meet me to-
morrow at the kadi's after the noon hour of
prayer, I will be there before you. Enter
boldly, demanding your pail, and I promise
you it will be returned to you."

The zealous Ahmed could gain no further
word from her, so went away greatly perplexed.

The next day Hajjeh Fatmeh arrayed herself in rich but somber robes, and, while from
the turret of the minaret the deep-toned voice
of the muezzin was still resounding in the ears

of a city's worshipers, sought the kadi's presence, thinking to find him in his luxurious court. The palace however was silent, save for the passing footsteps of those who, like herself, came to present their claims.

"His excellency has gone to the mosque to pray," said the guard.

"To those in grief, time does not hinder," answered Hajjeh Fatmeh, bowing her head and drawing her black veil more closely. "I will await his return."

The great man's devotions were protracted and many suppliants were gathered in the court to await him, but when at last he appeared, his countenance beaming with pious complacency, Hajjeh Fatmeh was the first to throw herself at his feet.

"O noble Kadi, at whose approach the very trees bow their heads in deference, I prostrate myself before you, the shadowing shade of refuge for all who are distressed. Be it known to you, O Kadi, exalted and excellent, that my husband, a merchant of great wealth, now in Bagdad, has sent me word that he has fallen sick and requires me to go to him at once to nurse him back to health. And, O most gracious Kadi, whose pity is like the sun shining upon the snows of Lebanon, you will surely understand that, though my grief at my Afendeh's illness is as the ocean in its depths, yet as the ocean, it obeys the voice of him who hath ordained it. But now my sorrow and perplexity come from a far more earthly source, even as all distresses wrought by man are harder to be borne than those that God has sent. My mind is rent with conflict what to do with my Afendeh's money, which he committed to my care before he left and which I dare not carry on the brigand-infested highroad to Bagdad. I seek a man of undisputed honesty with whom to leave the treasure. But honest men are rare, and few know this more truly than you, O most august of kadis, whose dealings with the sons of men are as the multitudinous divisions of watercourses among the irrigated fields. Therefore, I have come to you, even as the bee to the honey-laden flowers of henna, that I may gain your wise advice and learn where I may find a man of perfect honesty."

As the kadi listened, his face beamed more and more with satisfaction, and, rubbing his hands, he asked: "What is the sum you wish to place?"

"Twenty thousand liras,"* answered Hajjeh Fatmeh, "and few men can be trusted with such a sum."

"I think we shall have no trouble in finding such a man," answered the kadi, stroking his beard and puffing hard through his argileh to hide his eagerness.

"But I should wish to see proof of his honesty," said Hajjeh Fatmeh.

Just then, the pilgrim Ahmed entered and prostrating himself before the kadi said, "I come to ask your Excellency for a pail of treasure which I entrusted to your care seven months ago."

"Certainly, certainly," said the kadi. "Guards, bring the pail at once from my treasure-house." Forthwith the pail was brought and given to Ahmed and the kadi turned with an inquiring look to Hajjeh Fatmeh.

Just then a shrill song of joy, the *zlaghit,* was heard and Hajjeh Fatmeh's maid entered, dancing.

* A Turkish lira has a value of $4.40.

"The Afendeh, Hajjeh Fatmeh's husband, has returned, cured of his sickness!"

Hajjeh Fatmeh joined her in the zlaghit. Then once more bowing to the kadi, she said, "Since Providence has thus ordained, I need no longer journey to Bagdad, and hence will not require further to trouble your Excellency."

She left the court, followed by her maid and the pilgrim Ahmed with his pail.

VIII

A LIFE BEHIND
A VEIL

I WAS born in the sunny south of France, but early in life I became governess in the family of a French consul and sailed with them to Syria. I came greatly to enjoy my life in one of the far-away seacoast cities, with its cheerful amphitheater of gardens and red roofs rising above the blue expanse of bay, and the snow-topped Lebanon shining in tints of purple and pink and silver over all.

At the end of two years, when my patrons left, I decided to remain. I had learned something of the language and ways of the people, and soon gained the position of companion to the daughter of Kamil Afendeh, a rich Moslem gentleman of the city. My charge Selimeh was a fascinating young thing, plump and fair-skinned, with brilliant brown eyes and black hair. She had attended during her childhood one of the European schools in the city. She had worn a hat and European dress and had been allowed the same freedom as her schoolmates. But for some time these things had ceased; she was now sixteen and of course could not go out of the house alone, nor without her izar * to cover her from head to foot. I saw quickly that these things chafed her. I found her one day smiling before the mirror in my room with my hat on.

"You will not mind," she said in her pretty, coaxing way, "if I sometimes wear it here indoors; it makes me feel free again."

We went away soon after this to a mountain village to spend the summer. I shall never forget Selimeh's naïve pleasure over the new experience of traveling by train. The railroad had just been opened and was to all a marvel of almost supernatural power. Our family party just filled a compartment, so Selimeh could give full vent to her spirits. She was

* A long veil-like outer garment, worn by Moslem women.

charmed with the rapidity of motion, even when
the cogs crept up the mountainside at the rate
of seven kilometers an hour. With the gayety
of a small child, she would raise and lower the
window every few minutes, with fresh exclama-
tions of rapture over each change of scene.
We passed the fertile plains of olive, apricot,
and pomegranate orchards, up through the
spicy pine groves of the foot-hills, to the bare
flanks of Lebanon. Mountainsides of purple
rock met each other, with roaring torrents between. It was all wonderful to me: in my cultivated France, all nature is a garden-bed,
every portion used for man's benefit; but here
was a rude wastefulness which seemed to despise petty human frugalities.

We reached the half-way station at the hour
of prayer. Kamil Afendeh and his son took
out their prayer-rugs, spread them upon the
platform, and proceeded as usual with their
genuflections and prostrations. They were
only half through when the whistle sounded for
starting; the passengers returned to their
places. A second signal was sounded. The
younger man cut short his devotions and returned to his place. Not so the father; sol-

emnly he raised his hands to heaven, then knelt and kissed the ground. A third bell was rung.

"Ya Afendeh!" cried the guard. "Ya Afendeh! the train will start without you!"

But not until he saw the compartment doors being shut did he shuffle into his shoes, pick up his rug, and hasten back to his place, muttering as he ran the last sentences of the prayer.

Our summer among the mountains was a delight. We looked down a green valley, held in by ridges of rock, to the shining city by the sea. Between stretched a mist of olive groves, hemmed in by the border of sea sand, the living thing in our landscape. It glowed and trembled in the intense sun-heat and became now golden, now dull brown, now a burning red, like a stream of molten metal. Beyond all glittered the blue and silver sea. This was our day view.

At night a spell fell upon our world. At sunset we would see a line of white mist stretched along the horizon; as we watched, this would unfold itself like a canopy, cover the sea, rapidly expanding toward us, till the whole plain was shut out of view; then creeping up

the valleys, it would wrap around the feet of
the outlying ridges like billows around a prom-
ontory. When the moon rose, it would be upon
a phantom ocean with a phantom shore. But,
even as we watched, the billows would be dissipated and the whole level sea melt away, and
from its depths would again shine out the
twinkling lights of the plain.

Every day the ladies of the family flocked
out in a gay bevy to walk. When we were beyond the village limits, veils were thrown back
and we enjoyed our freedom. Most of the
ladies preferred sitting by the stream for passive enjoyment; they would roll their cigarets
with the skill of adepts, chattering and laughing between the puffs of smoke. Selimeh and
I chose instead to climb over the rocks, where
overhanging maidenhair and grasses revealed
the trickling streamlets, and the spicy odor of
henna intoxicated the senses.

One day the whole party roamed down into
a glen below the village, where walnut-trees,
cane, and bramble made an alluring tangle.
The ladies' veils trailed back carelessly from
their girdles, and with something of the freedom of the mountain maidens they started

scrambling across a narrow path. We heard a slight shriek from the foremost one, and saw to our consternation, directly in front of us, a young man, a gentleman whom I rec)gnized at once as Rashid ul-Hassan, one of the rising young men of our city. A dilemma indeed! Unveiled ladies, a narrow path, and a gentleman directly before us! With an inspiration worthy of his code of etiquette, the young man turned his back to the path and stood facing a rock till the party had passed! On our return, Kamil Afendeh was so much pleased with the deference thus paid to his harim, that he sent a basket of fruit to the young man in acknowledgment of his delicacy. But I knew better. I had noticed the quick glance, all-sufficient, which had glowed upon Selimeh and only Selimeh, and I knew that something had begun.

The summer passed, the first rains of autumn fell like a blessing, carrying away the dust and disease of the four months of dryness. We were again in the city. It was pleasant after all, we thought, to be once more in touch with throbbing life. My love for the modes, which has always been my chief weakness, led

me again into my favorite street, among the
European shops. I was turning home one
afternoon with my purchases, when some one
stepped up to me from behind.

"I beg pardon, mademoiselle;" the accents
were of the most fluent French. I recognized
at once the lithe figure with its European dress,
and the consideration of manner, which seemed
to be habitual.

I bowed gravely, but let my eyes smile, as I
answered: "I think I have had the pleasure
before of seeing—your back."

Rashid ul-Hassan flushed. "It is about that
occasion that I have taken the liberty of speaking to you." He looked uneasily at the crowds,
Syrians, Bedouins, Europeans, who thronged
back and forth before us.

"In a crowd one is most alone," I said.

"Thank you," he answered. "In our land
we can use only such opportunities as we
have." Then he was silent.

I waited. He gathered himself together
again.

"Mademoiselle, I may speak freely to you;
you know the honor and freedom of the West,
where men and women know and trust each

other. Since that day last summer, there has
grown upon me a necessity; it is an honorable
and manly wish, that would not be denied me
in your country; may I look to you for help?"

I knew what was coming.

"I must see Mademoiselle Selimeh again;
I must speak to her."

I tapped my parasol nervously upon the
stone pavement. He went on more eagerly.
"My grandfather keeps a silk shop in the
bazaar; take her there. We shall meet accidentally."

Something of the spirit of the old trouba-
dour days leaped within me. I knew that what
he asked was but a common right of human
beings. I knew moreover that my Selimeh had
lost all her childish pleasure in life ever since
that time.

"I am but the necessary instrument of fate,"
I said to myself. "I will go with her," I spoke
slowly, "at the time you name."

"To-morrow morning," he answered eagerly.
"I am eternally your debtor."

I did not tell my plot to Selimeh; she consented readily enough to a shopping foray on
its own merits. We passed the European

streets, blockaded with carriages, thronged with fashionably dressed people, and entered through a low archway the bazaar of the old city; through one archway from the twentieth century to the Middle Ages! We found ourselves in an open court alive with a moving multitude, gay with ever-shifting colors, ringing with the calls of the traffickers.

"*Ya Karim!* O Thou Gracious One!" cried the vendor of fresh loaves. His meaning, mystical to a stranger, was evident to those who heard: "God, the Gracious One, supplies you with bread."

The sherbet-seller tinkled his brass cups, and poured out cool drafts for passers-by. The aged tinman sat in the door of his shop patiently converting old kerosene tins into cups and coffee-pots. The potter sat among his jugs and smoked in silence.

"Allah will send the customers," he said to himself.

Selimeh and I picked our way up a slippery paved alley. We were pushed back upon a wall as a string of loaded mules passed by, and were much encumbered by a growing cortege of beggars. But the silk bazaar was not far off. We found the aged merchant sitting alone in his shop, enjoying the soothing bubble of his argileh. He saluted us with portly dignity. An attendant brought chairs and called the sherbet-seller from the street. Two cups were filled and brought to us overflowing in honor of our dignity. But these were only common courtesies accorded to customers of rank; I had no reason to suppose that our plot was known.

We explained what silk we wanted. With much deliberation the old man hunted among his wares and spread the goods upon the counter. Selimeh was delighted.

"The venerable gentleman will excuse you," said I, "if you throw back your veil; you cannot see to choose."

With the impatient toss of her head, which she always gave handling her veil, Selimeh threw it to one side. Her cheeks were flushed, her eyes shining with unusual brilliance. But the old gentleman did not readily follow her fancies, as she tossed aside one piece after another of his rich goods.

A door opened. "I think I can find what the lady wishes," said a voice, and young Ras-

hid ul-Hassan entered. Selimeh started and
drew her veil in confusion.

"I beg pardon," said the young man, in
French.

Strange that the mere foreign accents should
carry with them a code of life, but as the goods
were displayed and the trifling remarks and
explanations made in regard to them, Selimeh
became quite naïve and self-forgetful; indeed
it seemed to me she was hardly careful to keep
her veil in place. That was all, but in that
paltry interview a social system was defied.
When we reached home, Selimeh was very
silent.

"What have I done!" thought I, and trembled.

A short time after this there was a great stir
in the family. The brother and uncle of Rashid ul-Hassan came to Selimeh's father and
formally requested that she should be Rashid's
bride. Kamil Afendeh would not hear of the
proposition.

"For months I have destined my daughter
to a far more honorable position, to be the
wife of Said Afendeh, the wealthy and re-
nowned."

"But Said Afendeh is old and ugly, and has a wife already," shrieked Selimeh.

"What is that to you?" said her father. "Does not our holy law ordain that man shall have four wives for his portion?"

Selimeh pressed her lips together. "You may bury me alive," she said, "but you cannot marry me to Said Afendeh."

Coaxing, threats, tauntings were tried, but my warm-blooded, high-spirited Selimeh seemed suddenly turned to stone. She was shut up in a room by herself, with only a piece of sacking to sleep on. I wept, I besought for her, but I soon saw that if I were not discreet, I should be sent away.

One day, we heard a commotion in the street, several shots were fired. Presently Selimeh's mother came in, carrying a bloody handkerchief and a fez pierced with a bullet hole, and showed them to Selimeh.

"Tell me whose these are," she said.

Selimeh sank down upon the floor. I looked at the name on the handkerchief; it was indeed Rashid ul-Hassan. I wondered how Selimeh would live through it; but grief seldom kills. I was now allowed to be with her again. She would sit most of the time leaning her head upon my lap or shoulder, speechless, motionless.

I tried one day to interest her in the sunset. We had had a storm, and sea and sky were leaden black; one shaft of sunlight broke across the bay and struck the ships in the harbor, bringing them out from the gloom like ships of fire. Selimeh looked out of the window with me. Suddenly she caught my arm and pointed to the street. I looked down and saw Rashid ul-Hassan! Selimeh was very white.

"Go and speak to him," she said.

I ran down breathless and surprised him much. "We thought you were dead," I said.

He looked amazed. I told the story of the fez and handkerchief; his eyes darkened with a dangerous look as he listened.

"I was out of the city," he said, "when that low street quarrel took place; that handkerchief was stolen from me by some base trick."

I went back to Selimeh and found her trembling on the floor. I told her of the conversation, then left her before my courage should fail for a bold resolve. I went straight to Kamil Afendeh.

"Your daughter will die," I said, "if you do not let her marry Rashid ul-Hassan." I did not wait for his answer.

I spent a night of sleepless suspense. Early in the morning my reward came. Kamil Afendeh came into the room where Selimeh, her mother and I were sitting, and said:

"I have decided to give my daughter to Rashid ul-Hassan; be ready for the wedding in ten days."

It seemed too wonderful to be true. Selimeh went about the house in a sort of trance, while the rest of us worked ourselves into a fever over satins, laces, and embroideries. Of course, the bridegroom did not visit his bride; that would be a liberty unknown in our society. But Selimeh was satisfied.

She came to me one day and said: "How strange that I should be so happy, when so many others are miserable!"

"What is it now?" I said.

"I was down-stairs with the washerwoman, Khazma," she said, "and found her crying; I asked her what was the matter. She answered that her husband's brother had been beating her. 'Of course,' she said, 'we expect our husbands to beat us, but it is hard when our husbands' brothers begin it too.'"

"What did you say?" I asked, half laughing.

"I comforted her as well as I could," said Selimeh, "I put my arms round her and kissed her wet face, and said I hoped in the future no one would ever beat her, except her husband."

Soon after this came the wedding festivities. Our house was given up to the women, who flocked to the place swathed in izars. They decked Selimeh and sang her songs of praise and smoked in her honor all day. In the evening, we were packed into carriages and taken to the house of the bridegroom. That also was crowded with women. Selimeh was greeted with acclamation and seated in honor upon a divan. Throughout the evening the women danced and sang before her and refreshed themselves with coffee and sweets.

The bridegroom and all the men were assembled enjoying their own festivities in the house of one of the bridegroom's friends. At midnight, a commotion arose in our court.

"The bridegroom has come!"

The guests made a feint of covering their faces and Selimeh was draped in a thick veil.

Her mother and I, with women relatives, waited with her in our side room. We heard footsteps, as the bridegroom and his brother were ushered to the head of the court. We could tell that the bridegroom was now seated and waiting for his bride to be brought to him for the fateful raising of her veil. Selimeh held my hand tight and trembled as she waited.

"We must start now," said her mother. The women closed round her. I rose to join them.

"No, you must remain here," said her mother decisively.

I looked at her in amazement. "I am your daughter's constant companion——"

But already Selimeh had been swept out of my reach and a group of relatives crowded round me with emphatic assertions that I must not see the ceremony. My mind grew confused with the unexpectedness and strangeness of it all. Suddenly I heard a scream. I broke through the group of women and ran to the court. Selimeh lay upon the floor senseless. Beside her stood, not Rashid ul-Hassan, but Said Afendeh. The demon plot was all clear now.

"We must take her home!" I cried. "This is not the bridegroom!"

A hand was clasped tightly over my lips. "He is her husband; he has lifted her veil." It was Selimeh's mother who spoke.

We laid Selimeh upon the divan and something was poured down her throat; it kept her insensible for a time. I was ordered to leave the house, but on my entreaties was allowed to remain on condition that I should make no disturbance.

I went back to my Selimeh and covered her with my kisses and tears.

"Do not cry," she said. "Selimeh is dead."

Early the next morning, I saw a white figure glide past my door toward the piazza; it looked like Selimeh. A sudden fear seized me; I threw on my robe and followed. There was no one there! With a sick apprehension I looked over the railing to the street. A crowd was already gathered round a motionless white figure. They carried her up and laid her on her bed. The news went rapidly through the house; the women screamed and ran about in a frenzy. Selimeh's mother came; we left her alone with her dead child.

I could not stay away long; I came back to stand outside the door. What was my horror to hear shrill singing within. I opened the door; the mother had decked Selimeh's head with flowers and had spread her wedding dress over her; she was dancing beside the bed singing the wedding song and shrieking by turns. I was shocked beyond measure and tried to draw her away, but she only cried the louder: "This is my daughter's wedding day!"

The women drew me into the court.

"Let her alone," they said. "This is our custom; when young people die, we make a wedding for them."

That afternoon they carried her away. The hired mourners beat their breasts and shrieked; the women of the house flung their arms into the air, crying, "Farewell! Farewell!" But above every sound in the babel of hopelessness rose the mother's wedding song.

A SOFT sea-breeze was fluttering in upon the Syrian coast, bending low upon its way to catch the whisper of the water as it rose to the brim of ragged crevices, to sink again amidst a dripping fringe of seaweed. The breeze carried the dreamy murmur through the open doorway of a fisherman's hut and the sound came like a far-away memory to the aged Abd-ur-Rahman, who lay upon his pallet on the floor.

"This is the last time, my daughter," said he, "that I shall ever see the pink sunset light upon this water."

Zahra bent over her father's hand, kissing it passionately. "You will bury me, O my

101

father! Do not speak so! How could I live without you?"

"Yes, my daughter, it is the burning of my heart that I must leave you uncared for; but the vow that has cut you off from the world and the married life has given you to God; he is gracious."

"O father! do not think that I ever regret the vow. I remember so well from the time that I was a child when first my little sister and then my little brother died, and I knew even then, because every one said so, that it must be my fault, that I, poor unfortunate child, in spite of my great love for them, had somehow brought the evil eye* upon them. And oh! how miserable I was! And, when little Aziz was born, I remember how terribly the thought came over me that perhaps, against my will, I should bring the evil eye on him too and make him die like the others. And I went to my grandmother and asked her to hang another charm around his neck, and I would hardly look at him lest I should bring the 'eye' upon him, but instead, whenever I felt a great longing to take him up

* The supposed power of harming by spiteful looks; much dreaded in the Levant and the East in general.

and love him, I would run away and hide
among the rocks and cry my heart out. And
you and my mother saw that I kept away from
him and thought I hated him and felt sure that
this would attract the evil eye still more. I
remember you spoke of taking me to the Holy
Well and letting me down in it to dissipate the
evil influence, and then you thought of dressing
me in black and leaving Aziz's hair uncut until
he was seven years old, but you finally decided
that all these things were too slight to avail. It
was at the time of the great Sacrifice of the
Dahiyeh, when so many thousands of sheep are
offered, that you said to me, 'My daughter, you
must be the sacrifice for your brother.' And
then you made the vow, so unusual for a Moslem, the *Nathr,* like the vow of the Christian
nuns, that I should be set apart from the world
and should never marry like others, but should
be forever a Nazarite. It is this that has kept
him alive, father; it makes me so proud and
glad to know it, and that my life has been a
ransom for his."

"Yes," said her father, "but you have done
still more. When your mother died so young,
you took her place; I can see you now, when

little Aziz came home from school, taking his
red calico bag of books off his shoulder and
washing his feet, then pulling out the bread-
trough from under the divan and giving him
the bread-cake in which you had tucked a morsel of cheese or some olives. And then, when
he would bring his troup of little cousins in to
supper, you would seat them in a circle on the
floor and set the dish of red lentil pottage in
the midst; and, as you watched it disappear so
fast, you would take your own dry loaf and eat
it by yourself out on the rocks. Do not think
these things escaped me. And what did it all
come to?" The old man's face grew white with
anger, and, lifting himself upon one elbow, he
raised his trembling right hand to heaven.
"The Lord return upon him seven times his
wickedness and his ingratitude! He for whom
you gave up your life, for whom I worked night
and day on the wet rocks with the winter winds
cutting against my half-naked body! He, who
never brought one piaster to his old father, but
spent all he had in his revelings in the cafés!
That he should turn against us and leave us,
cursing his father and his sister and their religion! May the Lord cut him off——"

"Father, father, do not say the words!" cried Zahra. "Do you know, sometimes I blame myself, and think, if I had not always indulged him but had sometimes punished him when he did wrong, he might have been more thoughtful of others." Then she checked herself. "What words for me to say! No, no! If he were back here now, I should do only ten times more, and if he asked for anything, I would give my two eyes to get it for him."

"That is what *he* ought to do for you," answered her father, "now that he has become prosperous in Tyre. When I vowed you a Nazarite, I expected of course that your brother, for whom you were cut off from other support, would take you to his home."

"What a joy that would be!" exclaimed Zahra. "How I would serve him and his wife! Indeed they would never have cause to regret my coming."

"But as it is," went on her father bitterly, "what can you do to put a morsel of bread into your mouth?"

"I have thought about it much," answered Zahra. "I hoped at one time that I might make something by selling salt; so I poured sea-water into little hollows on the surface of the rocks and watched day by day for the sun to dry off the water and leave the crust of salt for me to gather, but the soldiers saw me and threw dirt on my salt and of course they had the right, as I was going against the law." She sighed. "At any rate, my trial gave me one idea, that I might at least knead my bread with sea-water and that would save my having to buy any salt. Perhaps I could learn to spin silk; if I worked at it from morning till night, I might earn twenty paras* a day. I could sometimes carry bread to the public oven for the neighbors and they would give me a bread-cake for doing it. But some day I shall grow too old for work, perhaps I may go blind; so many do. Then I shall have to sit by the side of the street and spread a handkerchief before me on the dust, putting four pebbles on the corners to keep it from blowing away, and, per-haps, when the people pass, Allah may soften their hearts and they may sometimes drop a copper for me."

Both were silent for a long time.

Zahra suddenly broke out in a changed,

* Twenty paras have a value of about two cents.

brightened tone: "Do you remember what my uncle told when he came back from the far-away countries, from the Land of Barazil and the Land of Noy Yurk and the Land of Chi-cako, that there women have almost as many ways of living as men; they come and go without veils, and work in factories and keep shops, and some learn how to write on paper and earn their bread by it, but I can hardly believe this. But the strangest thing of all he said was that there the unmarried women are of equal honor with the married ones! And they often even prefer not to marry at all!"

Her father looked grave. "Do not believe all you hear, my child; there are many lies in the world."

He seemed deep in thought for a while; at last he spoke: "Do you remember, Zahra, how often when you were a child, I used to take you with me in my fishing-boat and when I had spread my nets, you used to help me throw out wheat upon the surface of the water to attract the fish? I remember the first time that I took you that you said, 'Isn't it a shame, father, to waste our precious wheat? This is our bread!' But I told you to wait, and the next day I took you back to the place and there were the nets full of fish! Our bread had returned to us in double measure. Now, Zahra, your life has been spent in casting out precious wheat; surely he who rules the earth and sea will bring it back to you in peace."

His voice was weakening rapidly.

"O father, give me your blessing," pleaded Zahra.

He put his hand upon her head. "In the name of God," he murmured.

Zahra raised her wet face with a rapt look. "O father, give a blessing to Tyre also, to Tyre, O my father!"

She threw open the southwest window and let in the glorious sunset light.

"Stretch out your hands toward Tyre, father."

She kneeled beside him again, her eager face bright with the reflected splendor. The lines about the old man's face worked painfully; then a softness seemed to come over him. Raising himself with difficulty, he stretched out his two hands toward the open window and breathed between his sobs: "My blessing and my forgiveness, O my son."

The long talk had exhausted him and he wearily closed his eyes and Zahra sat down upon the doorstep with head bent upon her knees.

She was roused presently by her aunt, Im Ali, from the neighboring cottage. A fat, flabby creature in flimsy blouse and red Turkish trousers, but with head carefully veiled, her appearance was not prepossessing; neither was her voice, which was shrill and coarse and drawn out with a peculiar falling inflection distinctly feline. But there was something not unkind in her manner as she shook her niece from her reverie.

"Destroy your courts! What are you doing here? W'Allah, you look pale; you have not slept for eight days."

"How can I sleep?" sighed Zahra. "Father thinks he is not going to live."

"Oh, far removed be the evil!" exclaimed her aunt. "By the cutting off! are you going to believe every whim of a sick person? W'Allah, an hour ago, he looked better to me than I have seen him for fifteen days."

"Oh, please talk softly," said Zahra. "He is asleep."

"Never fear," replied her aunt, dropping her voice mysteriously, "what I want to say must go no farther than your ear. Get me the argileh and I will talk to you here."

Zahra filled the glass bottle with water, adjusted the tobacco and a bit of glowing charcoal at its mouth and handed the long stem to her aunt.

The woman drew the smoke thoughtfully for some moments, staring at the bubbling water as though for an inspiration.

"Zahra," she said at last, "you know you are a Nazarite."

Zahra smiled; "I am not likely to forget that."

"And far be it from me," continued her aunt, "to belittle the sacredness of the vow. When your father made it, I was the first to approve, and I never stopped telling your brother that it was you who preserved his life and that he owed it to you to care for you. But what has he done? Cursing and reviling us all in the name of our religion! The Lord reward him! Zahra, he has cut himself off from mercy; Allah will never require it of you to sacrifice yourself any longer for him!"

"Oh, do not say any more," cried Zahra. "My vow is the most precious thing in the world to me; with it I have bought a life!"

"W'Allah, you must listen," said her aunt. "It is a question of your living or dying. Whom have you in the world when your father is gone? Here am I, your only relative, tied hand and foot with my big family, and my husband a poor man. We would never deny you a morsel while we have it, but sometimes we have not food for our own children. Can we eat the soil and wear the walls of the house?"

"I should not ask you to support me," said Zahra.

Her aunt continued: "You know the proverb, 'God strikes with one hand and protects with the other.' And he has now sent you what you could not have expected, being a Nazarite; he has sent you the lot of all others."

Zahra was sobbing upon her knees. "Yes, I know who it is. Please do not say anything more about it."

"You know!" exclaimed her aunt. "If you had seen him, what a fine handsome man he is, and if you knew his good position and reputa-tion——"

"Yes, I have seen him," said Zahra, but added quickly, "of course, I did not speak to him, nor he to me. It was when I took my jar to the well; I suddenly came face to face with a stranger; I drew my veil quickly, but I saw his face, he was what you say. Of course, I did not know then, at least, why should I think so? but just now when you told me, I felt sure this must be the one."

"Yes, it must have been," said the aunt. "There is no other stranger about. But he is not unknown to us. He is from a good family; his name is Hamad Jafar. He has heard all about you and about the vow, but he does not mind. He asks me to take you with him to the sheikh in the city, and the writing will be written and you will be his legal wife; after that, the world can say nothing."

"Yes, and then my brother will die," said Zahra solemnly. "No, tell him I cannot think of it," and she rose proudly and went back to her father.

Im Ali followed her and struck a light, suddenly revealing the wanness and haggardness of the sick man's face. The woman's heart smote her with horror: "Here I am trying to

marry off the girl and my own brother is dying!
The poor, poor child, how can she see him——"
and with reeling brain Im Ali tried to busy
herself about the room.

She presently beckoned Zahra out again.
"Praise be to Allah," she said. "See how much
better your father is! Now I am going to stay
with him to-night and you go and sleep in my
house; you will come back to find him well in
the morning. Go ask your cousin to give you
the cup of coffee that I left for you."

Zahra objected at first, but she was too much
exhausted to hold out long.

Her aunt watched her disappear with evident relief. "I hardly thought I could get her
off so quickly, but Allah inspired me; the
sleeping-draft will keep her quiet now. It
is only kindness to keep her away—O my
brother, my brother! how can I let you go!"
and she beat her portly chest with sincere grief.
"O Death, may your own life be cut off!"

Interested neighbors soon dropped in, as
usual in times of sickness, and for each new-
comer Abd-ur-Rahman made a fresh effort to
raise himself on his bed. The excitement and
confusion, with the suffocating air of the room,

were tiring him out, but it did not occur to any one to let him remain quiet.

At last the timid click of a staff against the stones outside announced the arrival of the blind sheikh who had been called to perform his religious offices for the sick man. The sheikh entered, a picture of dignity, in his long robe and turban, his sightless gaze full of devout resignation.

"There is no God but God," he uttered in a sonorous tone, and then followed the lengthy intonation of sacred passages. Few could understand the words, so transformed they were by inflections and rhetoric, but the doctrine was presented rather by impressiveness of tone and manner than by words, the stern doctrine of the fatalist, of submission to the all-powerful, overwhelming God.

Before the words were ended, Abd-ur-Rahman had passed beyond the reach of human voice.

As soon as the company realized the change, the little hut became a turmoil of lamentation, shrieks, and wild running to and fro, lasting for hours, while preparations were made for the hasty Oriental funeral.

But through it all the mystic draft held its power and Zahra slept. Her aunt, thankful to have her plan succeed, waited till the last offices were performed and the last gift laid beside the dead, the earthen bottle of water, the seven cakes of fresh bread with the seven cakes of dry and the lump of henna, symbol of purity. It was now dawn and she availed herself of a lull in the wailing to pick her way among the projecting mulberry twigs to the closed door of her own hut. She entered noiselessly, but the motion was enough to dispel the remaining effects of the draft. Zahra raised herself in bewilderment.

"I have come to tell you good news," said her aunt; "your father is better and the neighbors have been coming in to congratulate him. So, if you hear any confusion of voices, do not disturb yourself—you ought to rest here awhile longer."

Zahra lay back again with a happy smile and her aunt left her, closing the door behind her.

Half an hour later the procession started from Abd-ur-Rahman's door, and a great cry rose from the assembly. A moment more and the figure of a girl, frantic with grief, head and face unveiled, rushed across the field and threw herself into the midst of the company. With the authority of grief, she commanded the men to let down the bier and they obeyed.

She threw herself beside it in a paroxysm of cries: "O father, father! Why did you not take me with you?"

They tried to draw her away, but she clung on still more wildly: "O father, take my message of peace to my mother, my message of peace."

The forty days which followed were a blank of bewilderment to Zahra, her one definite act being her daily visit to the dreary burying-place. She tenderly gathered day by day fresh myrtle branches while her aunt cherished with unwonted care the marigolds and pink carnations in the tin boxes at her door-step, gathering the flowers each day into a tight little bunch and dropping honest tears upon the strips of rag with which she wound the stems. The two women would make their way together to the dismal place—an unenclosed waste of sand, with only a bunch of thorns here and there among the broken head-stones. There they

would throw themselves upon the ground, and
would lay their offerings in order and remain
until aroused by some other mourner like themselves, or until the cry of the jackals among
the rocks reminded them that night was coming.

One day Im Ali was kept at home by the
illness of her child and Zahra was obliged to
go alone. Never had she felt so crushingly how
truly alone she was in the world. She sat wist-
fully watching the sparrows round a bit of
water in a hollow in the adjoining tombstone!
Their liveliness seemed to mock her. At last
she could bear it no longer, and started home,
her mind in a whirl.

It seemed to her that some one was following
her and she gathered her veil closer and quickened her steps. Presently she gave a little
scream; the person had caught up with her and
touched her on the arm. She knew who it was
before she saw him, the same stranger that she
had met at the well.

"Do not be frightened," he said. "I have
something for you; I could not trust it to any
one else." He drew out a paper and handed
it to her. "It is a letter from your brother."

"From my brother!" gasped Zahra; in all the time since he had left them, never had any message come from him before.

She opened it with trembling hands and looked at the signature.

"Yes, that is his name," she cried joyfully. "I remember how it used to look when he wrote it; he was so clever in everything."

She gazed at the closely-written lines above the signature eagerly, passionately, with the awe upon her face which the untaught always feel toward the written page.

"I cannot read it," she said, almost with a cry, and lifted her helpless beseeching gaze full upon his. In that moment the artificial restrictions of a lifetime counted for nothing, and it seemed in no way strange to either, this sudden sense of sympathy and comradeship.

"Shall I read it to you?" he asked.

She handed him the letter without a word and he read:

"To our honored and cherished sister, Zahra: May God prolong her life!

"After greetings and messages of peace, we write that the word of sorrow has reached us and that our heart is riven with anguish and desolation that cannot be comforted—to him whose power is over all be praise!

"And now we wish to commend to you our beloved friend Hamad Jafar, and be it known that he goes to you with our sanction and approbation and that you have our full and free permission to agree to all that he proposes; and we wish hereby to absolve you from all obligations brought upon you by a vow made many years ago; for we believe that its end has now been accomplished and its bond is now loosened by the power of the Gracious One in whose hands are all the events of our lives. And now with messages of peace to all who ask after our welfare, may you be preserved in health and safety.

"Your brother, Aziz."

Zahra listened with face buried in her hands, and after the reading had ceased, she remained in the same position, trembling and sobbing. Hamad Jafar stood with folded arms in silent respect until she grew calmer.

Then he spoke: "It was at my request that your brother wrote to you; you see he is my friend. I have spoken to your aunt again, and with your permission she has agreed to meet me with you to-morrow morning at dawn by the great rock that stands alone by the sea and we will go together to the city and make all right. Will you agree? Say the word."

"If God wills, I will agree, but give me time to think," answered Zahra softly.

"Forgive me for speaking," he said. "I know it is against the customs of our people; but our position is so peculiar. You did not know it, but I saw you in your grief at your father's funeral, and from that time I have felt as though I had always known you. My heart called out to you, 'Come to me!'"

Zahra hurried home with wildly beating heart; no wonder, in one moment to be swept from a past of self-renunciation, from a future of blankness, perhaps starvation, by this new strange possibility. Could human sympathy, companionship, love, be hers? She must have time to think. She turned off from the direct path, toward her favorite nook—a cavern joined to the sea by a rocky channel, through which the waves roared magnificently. She covered her face once more and seemed to see again Hamad's earnest look, with its pledge of sympathy.

When she raised her face again, it was with a new radiance of expression, and, stretching her two clasped hands toward the setting sun, she prayed:

"O God, when this sun rises, I may be no longer a Nazarite. Grant, oh, I pray, if I am doing wrong, that the punishment may fall on me, not my brother."

As her words ceased, a black cloud swept across the face of the sun, and, to Zahra's over-wrought mind, it seemed heaven's sudden answer to her prayer, an answer not of peace, but of warning and rebuke. She gazed trembling while a coldness and weakness crept over her and she fell upon the ground. It was long before she could think coherently, and when she rose, her face was gray with the gray twilight and her voice was dry and hollow.

"O God, forgive me," she murmured, "for even thinking of being untrue to my vow. I am going away now. Keep me and give me strength in the knowledge that I am still preserving the life of one so dear to me."

The next morning, when Hamad and her aunt came to the rock to meet her, Zahra had disappeared.

ENSIGNS UPON THE MOUNTAINS

Cedars of Lebanon

X

A LEBANON
RACHEL

LITTLE Rahil had been sent up the
mountainside to tend the goats. She
was now thirteen, a little young according to Western ideas, a little old according
to Eastern, to wander over Lebanon hillsides
alone. Probably the first Rachel, for whom
she was named, was about this age when she
went to water her father's sheep and met her
Jacob. Had Laban's daughter been older, it
is likely that she would have been kept at
home.

Rahil's goats wandered at large over the
mountain. They leaped from rock to rock, at
dizzy heights, holding their four feet together
and bending their pretty horned heads, while
deciding where next to alight. Their little

mistress, all unheeding, sat in the shadow of a
great rock, at her side a figure that had not
entered into the program planned by her
parents, a finely-built lad in hunting dress,
playing a shepherd's pipe. Rahil listened
dreamily.

Suddenly Amin threw down his pipe and
said: "Rahil, I am going away on a long hunting trip. You must not forget me while I am
gone. I want you to wear this till I come
back."

Amin fumbled in the folds of his blouse and
drew out a massive silver bracelet. Rather
awkwardly and shyly he put it upon Rahil's
arm. She turned scarlet and worked her bare
toes in the gravel. He knew, and she knew,
that all this was very improper.

"Rahil," continued Amin, "I should not say
this to you myself, but when I come back from
the hunt I am going to send my cousin to your
father, asking him to give you to me."

Rahil raised her head with a look as shy and
strange as that of her wild mountain goats.
"Do you forget," she said, "the quarrel between
your family and mine? If they knew that I
saw you here, they would kill me."

Amin sighed; then grew fierce. "Some day I will come and carry you away by force."

They sat on together for some time, neither saying much. Suddenly Rahil sprang to her feet in terror.

"See! the sun has set and I have not called my goats."

With loud, musical voice, she gathered the flock. They streamed down the mountain in a straight line, like a black cascade. Rahil could hardly count more than her ten fingers, but she noted with keen intelligence each familiar creature, as it bounded toward her, snorting a greeting to its little mistress. As the last one appeared, she wrung her hands.

"O Amin! the little one, the youngest, is not here; the bears will eat him and I am afraid to hunt among the rocks to find him." Amin looked delighted.

"No bears are a match for me. Wait and I will bring him." He took up the gun which he had thrown on the ground and scrambled nimbly up the mountainside. He had noticed that some of the goats had come down a steep fissure. He followed this up as it narrowed toward the summit, and soon heard the plaintive

call of the lost animal. He shouted to it reas-
suringly. It tried to come to him, but was held
by a bramble. He loosed it gently and tried
to soothe its wild panting as he carried it back.
He found Rahil almost as much frightened.
She took the creature eagerly from his arms
and carried it in her bosom. "Peace to your
hands and your feet," she said gratefully; "and
now I must go."

Amin once more seized the wrist that wore
the bracelet, kissed it fervently and hurried up
the mountain. Rahil bounded down the rocks,
her heart throbbing every moment more wildly
with fear.

It was dark when she gathered the goats into
the recess in the front part of the house and
stumbled over their black bodies to the open
living room beyond. The weather was growing
cold and Rahil's mother had built a fire of sticks
in the middle of the mud floor. She was now
stirring some onions in a frying-pan, placed
upon a coal grate at one side of the large fire.
The onion fumes, mingled with the smoke,
which tried vainly to escape from holes near
the ceiling, prevented the mother at first from
noticing Rahil. The child stood before her,

nervously twitching her ever-expressive toes.
She looked to the ceiling and noticed how black
the poplar beams were growing from the
smoke.

"O St. Elias!" she breathed, "when will my
mother look at me?" Her hand played with
the new bracelet concealed beneath her sleeve.
She did not notice that in her scramble down
the hill she had torn the sleeve at the elbow.
A silver gleam shot through the rent and
caught her mother's attention.

"Rahil, what have you there?"

"Nothing," said Rahil, pushing the trinket
up her arm.

"Your home be destroyed! You have,"
cried her mother, seizing her. Rahil struggled
and screamed; like a little wild animal she
kicked and bit in her rage, but the stronger
woman conquered and drew the bracelet off
Rahil's arm and hid it in the folds of her own
girdle.

"Who gave it to you?" she demanded, holding Rahil's wrists.

"My uncle's wife," said Rahil unblushingly.

"You liar! You daughter of a liar!" cried
the mother furiously, "you cannot deceive me.

That son of a dog, Amin, whose father insulted your father, has given it to you."

Rahil's childish figure straightened with the dignity of conscious right. She threw back her head and answered:

"Yes, Amin gave it to me, and he is coming afterward to ask for me."

Her mother shrieked, "For shame! for shame! Oh, that I had died without the disgrace of my daughter choosing a husband for herself!"

"Mother," pleaded Rahil, "do you not love my father?"

"Of course I do," she replied, "because he is my cousin. But I never saw him before we were married. I lived in Zaidan and he in this distant Ain Ata. When my father came home and said he had betrothed me to my cousin Selim, I covered my face with my veil and bowed my head and said, 'Let my parents do with me as they see best.' "

"But, mother, if you had liked some one else?"

Her mother cried aloud with horror, beat her breast, tore her hair and burst into a torrent of weeping. She crouched upon the floor, burying her face on her knees and swaying her body back and forth. Suddenly her husband appeared. She greeted him with a fresh shriek.

"What devil's performance is this?" he thundered. "Stop this noise and listen to me." The two women cowered in silence before him.

"I am tired of turning my house into Gehennem," he said, "and I have found a way to stop it. This morning Nakhi the muleteer asked me to give him Rahil for his son Mitri, so I went to my older brother's house and we called together all the men of the family and settled the matter. He wants Rahil in fifteen days, so you hurry and have things ready."

Rahil's face was blanched with dismay. "You cannot make me marry!" she cried. "I hate Mitri."

"You she-demon! Look out how you answer your father," he roared. "I am going back to your uncle's to tell him that all will be ready." He disappeared, discreetly dreading a struggle.

Rahil burst into frantic tears and threw herself at her mother's feet, kissing them and clasping them in her arms imploringly.

Her mother lifted her up. "My heart's beloved! My two eyes! Don't cry! I don't like Mitri either—oh, my child! This is your punishment for your boldness!"

Rahil clung to her. "Make my father change his word."

"If I only could!" groaned the mother.

When her husband returned, she entreated and wept—to no avail. He grew angry and struck her. He did not mean to be unkind, but women were ignorant and he knew no other way to restrain them. Rahil trembled in a heap on the floor.

The mother rose to take down the sleeping pallets of the family from the recess in the wall where they were piled. Once more she was choked with tears, the very mud plastering brought back a flood of recollection of their simple peasant life. Rahil herself had polished the floor and wall with a smooth stone till they shone like marble; together they had traced the patterns round the borders of the recess, and above was the elaborate lattice-work which the mother had woven with sticks and daubed with the clay that Rahil handed up to her. Crude reminders these of a witch of a maiden, smeared to the elbows and knees with mud; but the mother remembered the clear-cut olive face framed in its red kerchief, and she knew that there were no more shining brown eyes in Lebanon than those which looked up at her through tangled locks. The mother spread the pallets upon the floor and arranged the pillows and padded quilts; the family disposed themselves upon them, with no ceremony of altering their usual clothing.

Rahil lay motionless, with sobbing breath, for hours. The fire died down to a heap of embers, which glowed red against the streaks of blue moonlight breaking through the cracks of the door. Rahil watched the sleeping goats, surrounded with a warm steam from their own bodies; they helped more than the fire to heat the house. The air was suffocating, though she was not conscious of it. Why do the poor of all lands discard the one luxury free to them—fresh air?

Perhaps it was the closeness which at last became unbearable to Rahil. She slipped out from under her quilt, stepped carefully over the goats, and went out. The moon was glorious with a brilliance never seen in Western lands. Now that the fire was out of view, the moonlight looked no longer blue, but a rich gold; it poured upon the crags, and made them seem like enchanted beings starting from blackness of darkness. Rahil looked up to the mountainside where she had spent that beautiful afternoon.

"O sweet Virgin!" she gasped, beating her breast, "why must I be so miserable!"

She raised her arms with frantic eagerness toward the calm-faced moon, the pure naturalness of the motion more eloquent than words. With the abandonment of misery she threw herself full length upon the ground, her arms stretched out above her head. There her father found her at dawn, in the same attitude; he picked her up in his arms, numb from the cold, and in a state of mental apathy. He laid her tenderly upon her pallet and covered her well. She drank the herb concoctions which her mother poured down her throat, and let them do with her as they would.

"Rahil," said her father, "do you remember how often you have begged to visit your mother's family in Zaidan?"

"Yes," answered Rahil wearily.

"You know I always told you that it was too

expensive and too far away to send you, a whole day's journey."

"Yes," repeated Rahil.

"Now I have decided to let you go—if you will marry Mitri."

"I will do whatever you say, father."

"Nobly said, my child; I knew that my little girl would not willingly dishonor her parents."

He held out the back of his hand and Rahil kissed it, then raised it to her forehead, the act of submission taught to all Oriental children. And thus the child was bribed. Zaidan, a collection of flat-roofed houses, ranged like stairs upon the sides of a Lebanon gorge, was the metropolis of her little world, her Paris. She went, riding upon a mule, her sleeping-pallet over the pack-saddle, her wardrobe rolled up in a square of patchwork, hanging at her side. She came back to her lonely village dazed by the sight of many people coming and going, of the market-place crowded with gaily decked camels, with bales of goods, with display of fruits and sweetmeats. She carried back with her presents of raisins and fig-paste, and her grandfather's gift to her—a purple satin gown, brocaded with yellow flowers.

Then came the wedding. The house was a buzz of preparation for the entertainment of relatives from a distance. The paved yard resounded with the pounding of meat and dried wheat into a pulp for the favorite national dish—*kibbeh*. Vegetable marrows were scooped out and stuffed with savory rice and meat. Other portions of the rice were wrapped with infinite pains in the leaves of the grape-vine and cabbage. Over everything was a rich dressing of butter and fat. The cooking was all done over earthen grates out-of-doors, where space and light were available.

When the bride's veil was put on, she was made to fold her hands and close her eyes, and in this attitude she was kept for the greater part of eight days. A doleful imprisonment for the gazelle-footed child who had bounded all her life over the mountains! Her latent feminine vanity was her only solace. Truly this "being a bride" was the great occasion of her life, for which she and every other little girl in Syria had been brought up from babyhood; now for the first time in her life she was of some importance. She was the subject of these shrill songs of greeting which the women were chanting, and for her the men played musical instruments and danced outside. For the first time in her life, her dark blue rags were discarded; and for what magnificence! She patted the yellow satin on her lap and sighed to think how pleased Amin would have been to see her in it. If he were only here! Poor child! how could she know how hopelessly that yellow garment cut her off from the old life and associations!

She grew rather weary as the festivities wore on, and was glad when the last relatives rolled up their bundles for the morning's departure. All were busy, so she ventured to peep between her dark lashes. Oh, if she could only run out of doors! She looked toward the window and her breath stopped. There was no mistaking the haggard face and dark burning eyes, looking wild now. With a cry she reached out her arms and threw herself forward upon the ground in a paroxysm of weeping. Her mother and aunts sprang to her help, but could find neither cause nor remedy for the outburst. "Call old Im Shehin," said one; "she can cure her."

The hag soon came, with her herbs and

charms. She made a gesture of cunning with her forefinger.

"Listen to me; this is nothing but the evil eye. Get a scrap of clothing from the person who has bewitched her and burn the scrap."

"But she has seen no one," said the mother, going to the window; "not a soul has been near the house."

The old woman shook her head monotonously. "In any case, make her wear this blue bead around her neck; it will keep off the evil eye in the future."

In the evening a figure like a moving shadow sped away over the mountains above the village. What a contrast now from the day when last he leaped over these rocks and said good-by to little Rahil!

"I know she could not help it," he said fiercely, "I could see it in her eyes. They have torn her basely from me."

Amin reached his home sullen and moody. For months he refused to go with his old companions. His mother came to him at last with streaming eyes.

"My son, my only child, my soul! I can-

not see you grieving thus. You will not tell
me your trouble, and your father, God show
him mercy, is no longer living to help you.
But I have prepared the way for your happi-
ness; I have found you a bride."

Amin's response was a curse. But the
mother was not so easily daunted. Her father,
the uncles on both sides of the family, and
numerous cousins, in turn presented to Amin
the necessity of his becoming a householder in
his father's place. The thing was inevitable,
sooner or later; single life outside of a convent
is hardly to be thought of for a man or woman
in the East. So Amin consented.

The necessary feasting, smoking, and music
took their proper places. The bride was
brought, and for luck a lump of leaven was put
over the doorway as she entered. And the
new life began. Not a happy one it proved
to be. The gaily-decked bride soon developed
an unruly temper, which was vented first upon
her mother-in-law, later on, in hideous contrast
to the devotion of most Syrian mothers, upon
her own little daughter.

"She is a monster," thought Amin.

One day the woman became infuriated over

some trifle and struck the child. It was weeks before the little thing recovered, and Amin noticed that she was never strong again. When she was a year old she sickened and died. Amin could never rid himself of the thought that the blow had given some internal injury. After this, he took to drinking arak.* At the café he could at least listen undisturbed to the trickle of the rill of water through its stone trough. The sound of running water has an indescribable charm to the Oriental; so alluring it is that where water flows there carousals and fighting begin. One night Amin lingered and drank more arak than usual. His companions were discussing an expedition for the next day to the sacred grove of "Cedars of Lebanon," only a few hours' climb from their village.

"You know it is the feast of St. Jurjus tomorrow, so we shall be met by young men from Ain Ata, and have more arak and more fun." The speaker ended in a boozy song.

Ain Ata! Rahil's home! Amin had not heard mention of the place since that heart-

* A strong liquor used in the East, distilled from grapes.

sickening night of Rahil's wedding. He decided at once to join the expedition to the
Cedars. The thought whirled in his mind:
"Rahil's husband will be there;" but he had
taken too much arak to think coherently. He
reached his home after midnight, to find the
house in worse than ordinary disorder. His
wife, in an unusual effort at house-cleaning,
had pulled out earthenware barrels, wooden
boxes, and rude pieces of furniture from the
walls and left them in confusion. Amin stumbled over something as he entered; it was the
empty cradle that had belonged to their little
girl. Amin smothered a curse and made his
way to the pallet where his wife slept, and stood
watching her. Even in sleep, the lines of un-
governed temper were deep upon her face. A
sudden resolve came over him.

"I shall go away and never come back."

He turned quickly and left the house. He
half realized in his haste that he overturned the
earthen night lamp on the floor, but he did not
stop to make sure. He closed the door noiselessly behind him and stopped to think where
he should go first. Oh yes! there was that
appointment at the Cedars! He toiled over

the mountain all night and reached the grove
at early dawn, some time before the party from
his own village. He stopped to rest at the
entrance of the sacred enclosure. His instinctively religious mind was awed by the stillness
and darkness within, by the massive tree-
trunks, which had looked down perhaps upon
the workmen of Hiram, King of Tyre, and
still stood, columns in this great natural temple
of God. The trees spread out their arms, as
Amin thought, like one in prayer. The air
was heavy with the aromatic incense of the temple. Amin entered, and his footsteps fell
noiseless upon the springing carpet of cedar
needles. Suddenly a harsh sound cut through
the stillness, a coarse laugh.

"The party from Ain Ata is here before me,"
he exclaimed, hurrying toward them.

Before he reached them their hilarity had
turned into a dispute. He saw one of them
draw a knife. Heavens! It was Mitri, Rahil's
husband. Amin sprang upon him like a mountain leopard, caught the uplifted hand, and
turned the blow into Mitri's own bosom.

Amin sped away from the grove, but even
as he ran he shuddered with the thought, "I

have desecrated the Temple, the Temple of God!"

By a severe effort, he called back his presence of mind, and decided upon a way of escape. He turned his way toward the rocky ridges that led to the top of the Afka precipice. Years before, Amin had visited the world-famed Cave of the Adonis, at the bottom of the precipice. Gazing with reverent awe up the thousand feet of solid rock which tower above it, his eye had been arrested by a black line between two of the strata, half way up. After looking at it from different points of view he had made out a second cave, smaller than the Cave of the Adonis; and with a hunter's practised eye he had traced a possible path by which one might reach it from above. His observing keenness stood him in good stead now. Even Rahil's goats would have hesitated to try the path which he slung himself down. From stratum to stratum, on slippery ledges, that seemed barely a foothold for the mountain eagle, he at last worked his way to the cave. He threw himself upon the ground and studied the black walls.

"This must be my home for some time now."

He leaned over the edge and looked down a wall of five hundred feet to the roaring falls of the Adonis; then, grasping the tough stems of a bush at his cave's mouth, he hung back over the precipice, and looked up the five hundred feet of rock which he had climbed down.

"I shall have to learn that path well," he meditated. "I cannot bring much with me at a time."

He took out from his girdle his supper of bread and cheese which he had bought of some Bedouin Arabs in a high mountain valley on the way. His night's sleep was long and sound. In the morning he explored the inner recesses of his cave. There were many passages from two to four feet high, leading back into the mountains. He found that these communicated with each other and led into one or two main arteries. He followed the largest of these, on hands and knees, marking his way with peculiar groupings of stones, by which to trace his way back in the darkness. Suddenly the rocks seemed to open before him. He struck one of his much treasured matches and found himself in a marvelous rock palace. "A temple of stone!" he exclaimed. The walls glittered like diamonds, with here and there a seam of special brilliance. He struck another match and found that the gems were only drops of water. He did not recognize in them the wondrous power that had broken off the great limestone slabs at his feet, and carved out the grotto itself, but he spent his eager energies hunting for some little pool where the water might collect. He found it in a corner.

"Praise be to Allah!" he said devoutly, and drank deep of the water.

He soon came to feel at home in his cave dwelling. He learned to climb the rock path with ease and bought his slender supplies from the wandering tribes in the mountains. He might have lived there for months but for his one self-indulgence. The Oriental can hardly live without smoking. Amin ventured down after several weeks to the village of Afka to buy some tobacco. He was starting back with his supply when a man at the shop door seized him by the throat.

"You are my prisoner!"

Several others helped to hold him down, and Amin saw to his dismay, under the loose gown of his attacker, the police uniform. He was soon handcuffed.

"You double murderer!" cried the officer. "Is it not enough for you to kill a man, without putting an end to your wife too?"

"My wife!" gasped Amin.

"You need not pretend such innocence," answered the officer. "Bring him on, zabties!"

He was taken to the central prison. On the way he succeeded in falling back a step with his zabtie guard. He handed him half of the tobacco that he had bought.

"Tell me, the Lord lengthen your life, what do they accuse me of doing to my wife?"

The guard looked contemptuously at the lump of tobacco. "You bought twice that amount."

"Take it all," said Amin; "only tell me."

The guard carefully concealed the tobacco and explained. "On the morning of the Feast of St. Jurjus, some people passing your house saw smoke coming out under the door. They found the door unlocked and went in, but were almost overpowered with the fumes. When it had cleared a little, they found heaps of blackened and smoldering clothing and rubbish on the floor. Your wife was lying on her pallet at one side; the fire had not reached either her or the mattress, but the smoke had smothered her. People had seen you going to the house and leaving it the night before, so of course all know that you lighted the fire."

Amin bowed his head upon his breast. "Do they accuse me of anything else?"

"You fool! of course! Was it any other than you who killed Mitri of Ain Ata?"

"I did it, and saved another man, that he would have stabbed," cried Amin, indignantly.

"That very man swears that Mitri made no attempt to hurt him," said the zabtie.

"When perjurers are against me, there is no hope," said Amin.

He was sentenced to the murderer's penalty by Turkish law, fifteen years' imprisonment.

A year later there camped at Ain Ata a little company of strangers from a far-distant land, wearing a foreign dress and speaking a strange language to each other. The villagers flocked to see the sight and watch the busy preparations at the camp. The interest of the women was centered round a novel sight, a "Frangi" lady. Men had been there before in close-fitting black clothes with a stiff, round head-covering of straw or pith, but a woman of that strange race was a curiosity indeed. To their surprise, she greeted them in their own language. They clustered round her with a quaint mixture of curiosity and deference, examining her dress in detail, and scrutinizing her white hands, never guessing that she, on her part, was looking with unmixed admiration upon their own rich olive complexions and matchless eyes.

A little girl was patting the lady's hand. "You must wash yourself a great deal," she said. Another turned up the cuff of her sleeve. "Why, her arm is white all the way up!" Most of all they wondered at a small gold filling in her tooth.

"See how differently God has created these foreigners from ourselves!"

"Mariam, run and tell your grandmother to come and see a woman with a gold tooth."

"Oh, lady, please may we touch it?"

Some little girls busied themselves cracking walnuts and peeling off the brown coating of the kernels; then brought them, white and tender, to the lady. She accepted them graciously from the walnut-stained little hands.

"I wonder if you children are fond of stories," she said.

With exquisite simplicity, she told them tales of child-life long ago; of one who was hid in the rushes by a river; of another who was born in a wayside khan, whose cradle was a manger. The group slipped away at sunset; only one young woman remained, one with a sweet, sorrowful face, who had not spoken once.

"Lady," she said, "I am very unhappy, and it comforts me to listen to you. May I sit here with you? I have no one waiting for me at home."

"What is your name?" asked the lady.

"Your servant Rahil," she answered. "I used to be a happy child, but then strange things happened to me, and now my husband is dead and my little son, my only joy—O lady, may God send a son to you—my little son is dead."

The missionary looked through a mist across the mountains, toward the distant city, where in unhallowed ground, in the throng and discord of unchristian multitudes, she had left her own little one. The woman of culture and the peasant understood each other. The two talked long together. As she left, Rahil implored:

"Please send us a teacher to our village."

"It ought to be done," said the lady to her husband.

And so it was done the next winter. The Syrian teacher gathered a group of children into a dingy mud room in the village. Seated cross-legged in a circle on the floor they learned the perplexing elements of Arabic reading and, most of all, Bible stories and Bible words.

Most attentive among the scholars was Rahil. Her neighbors jeered, of course, but Rahil was too much in earnest to heed them. She applied herself with the passion of a strong nature and soon brought into activity a rare intelligence, undeveloped before for lack of mental food. When the Frangi woman came the following summer, Rahil told her joyously that she could now read.

"Then I must give you a *Towrah*" (Bible).

Rahil clasped the book with delight. The next winter the school could not be reopened, but Rahil now had her treasure secure. As years went by, she became the comforter of the sorrowful and lonely ones in her village, and many a time she would be called to see some sick one and read from the beautiful book.

The end of the fifteenth year came. Rahil sat musing on her rough stone doorstep. There was nothing in her immediate surroundings to attract, no mingling of trees and shrubbery among the houses, all glare and bleakness.

Rahil looked across the tiny enclosure of white clay and stones that formed her front yard. Beside her was the earthen jar that she carried twice a day to fill at the stream. A few cooking implements were also at hand. Her spindle lay unused in her lap. These things formed her life.

"And yet they are not my real life," she said to herself. Just then a shadow fell at her feet.

"Rahil, is this you?" The voice was the old voice.

"Amin! have you come to me from the dead?"

The sun fell full upon his face and seemed to glorify it. It was thus indeed that she had thought of him for all these years. A solemn silence, as of those who meet in another world, fell upon them both.

An hour later Amin drew from his bosom a book. "Rahil," he said, "you will find me changed. While I was in prison a man came to me with this."

"The Holy Towrah!" exclaimed Rahil, and running joyfully into the house, brought her own much loved volume and laid it in Amin's hand.

XI

A VILLAGE
ICONOCLAST

IN a remote valley among the Lebanon mountains, standing midway between arid gray cliffs above and lines of carefully cultivated green terraces below, gleamed a small, flat-roofed village church. From the awkward little belfry over the door the bell-rope hung down against the outer wall, and the small boys commissioned to ring for the service were delighting themselves with many unnecessary jangles as they pulled.

The people gathered slowly in the square of dust and stones before the church, forming into somewhat stolid groups, as people of a very uneventful life are apt to do. But there was a little stir of interest and deference at the approach of a striking figure, a man, tall and spare, leaning slightly upon his stick and clothed in the usual dark blue garments of the mountaineer, but distinguished even in the bending of his white head by the dignity of a thinker and in his clear-cut face by the purity of those who spiritually discern.

"That is Abu Nameh," said one, pointing him out to a stranger from a distant village. "He is the man who decides all our perplexities and settles all our disputes."

"I have heard of him," answered the stranger, trying to catch a last glimpse as the old man passed into the church. "They tell me that he is so holy that, when he walks abroad, the church bells ring of their own accord, and the sheep grazing on the uplands fall down upon their knees."

The villager continued warmly, "None has upheld our holy church and blessed saints like Abu Nameh, and may I never again see any one so broken-hearted as he was when his own son became a heretic."

"In the name of the cross!" exclaimed the stranger.

"You may call his son heretic," rejoined an-

other speaker, "if that is what his new doctrine
makes him, but I have been over to the mission
school to hear him preach, and I tell you, if
you wish to hear the holy words of a prophet
come back to earth, go and listen to Nameh,
son of Abu Nameh. His father still refuses
to go and hear him, but I know this, that Abu
Nameh spends all his days reading in his son's
Bible, and, give me your mind! you will some
day find that Abu Nameh is as much heretic
as his son."

The speakers were now swept forward into
the church with the rest of the people, and the
monotonously intoned service proceeded. Few
attempted to listen, some whispered together,
others stood with folded arms, passive, content
that their physical presence could insure them
a part in the general distribution of spiritual
blessings.

The final words of the service had melted
away, the little chorister-boy, with tense throat,
had warbled his last shrill "Kyrie eleison," the
cloud of heavy incense spreading over the
bowed heads of the congregation as one and
another knelt for a parting blessing before the
pictures of the saints.

Suddenly the hush was broken by a commanding voice: "Brothers, I have come to you
with a message from God."

All turned startled toward the speaker, none
other than Abu Nameh. He raised a hand
seamed and withered as a cactus-leaf at the end
of the long summer drought. "Brothers, last
night I saw a vision. I seemed to be walking
by myself over the hillside and I bent my steps
toward the church and entered and beheld a
wondrous sight. Around these walls were bent
in many sad and drooping attitudes the saints,
each gazing sorrowfully upon his own rude picture as a man may look into a glass to see his
face. And many in that holy company were
wringing their hands with grief, and I heard
cries of anguish and now and then I caught
such words as these: 'O Lord, how long? Wo
unto us that we, unwilling, should be the means
of drawing human prayer away from God!'
And all at once, as though by one deep, moving
impulse, they bent forward, each lifting up his
picture in his arms, and laden thus they glided
forward in a silent, strange procession. Passing through the doorway, they wound their
phantom way down by the foot-path leading to

the village sepulcher. I followed, filled with awe, and saw them reach the dreary hut, the door opening to them of itself, and they entered in the same unbroken line, and round the walls they placed their gilded pictures, facing the dead. This done, they swiftly drew together, and I seemed to feel the air move as they passed me, sweeping upward as a cloud to heaven."

Abu Nameh paused, his face intent with a rapt gaze, still beholding the glorious vision. "It is a heavenly message," he continued, in an altered voice as though speaking from a great distance, "I dare not disobey." Then, shuddering as though to call himself back to earth, he rang out the last words: "I cannot enter this church again until the pictures are taken away." He bent his head upon his breast and passed swiftly out.

The stir produced in the village by this remarkable discourse was without a precedent. Abu Nameh! The staunch upholder of holy tradition! What change was this? His only answer was, "Look in God's Book!" and the villagers, thus baffled, were thrown back upon the few among their number who could read.

Around the shops of these men of sudden eminence would collect a crowd of eager debaters, and passages were searched out and discussed with a keenness amazing to any one disposed to patronize the simplicity of the peasant.

To Abu Nameh himself it was a period of anxious perplexity. It was no small crisis for a man of his age to turn against what had always been to him most sacred. After his first bitter grief, years ago, over his son's embracing the simpler faith and worship (taught by the missionaries), he had given himself to the study of these questions, and year by year his vision had grown deeper, and he saw new truths unfold. True, they were colored by the teachings of the sect in which he had been reared, as one may see a landscape through the tinted windows of a church. Abu Nameh, loyal to his training and his generation, would never leave his sect. Of this he gave assurance to his people many times, and even his son, Nameh, child of the new dispensation, was content to have it so; the same church that had blessed him in his baptism should rear its cross above his sepulcher. But this same church, he assured his people with a seer's confidence, should change—had changed already through the heart-convictions of thousands of her followers; and, in the future, should she hope to lead their lives as she had led them in the past, she would have to throw aside the time-worn outer garments of her journey, that the impenetrable armor of her first faith might shine forth in its strength.

Weeks had now passed since Abu Nameh's message had been delivered, and the services which followed, deprived of his devout presence, seemed without a soul. It was the eve of the great annual feast, the celebration of St. Helena's finding of the true cross. Deep grief had settled upon the spirit of Abu Nameh, even the pain of estrangement from his own people, for this was the first time in his long life in the village that he should be absent from the solemn services of the Feast of the Cross.

His thoughts were far away, although he mechanically joined the family group assembled for the evening celebration on their flat housetop. On the roofs about them were other groups, all like themselves with a gathered heap of brushwood to be lighted in memory

of the signal-fires which carried St. Helena's
message of the finding of the cross at Jerusalem across the hilltops to Constantinople.
From the valley below rose the sweet discord
of many church bells, and presently the distant
fires began to twinkle out, one after another,
from the dusk, each with its red column of
smoke—the gathering constellations of light
marking the different villages of the valley.
Suddenly a crown of fire broke out upon the
summit of the opposite mountain, far above
the level of human dwelling, showing the fel-
lowship of the distant goatherds in the memorial.

Abu Nameh's grandchildren, despite their
Protestant rearing, soon had their own fire
cracking merrily, while they danced about it
like gleeful sprites. But the fitful light thrown
upon the face of Abu Nameh showed only an
expression of deepest pain. He watched the
red light die down at his feet and likewise the
smoldering sparks scattered over the valley,
and it seemed to him a type of his efforts to
enlighten his people. He was gazing sadly
into the embers, too absorbed to notice voices
below, when a little hand slipped into his.

"Grandfather, the men have come to tell you that they will celebrate the feast to-morrow by taking away the pictures."

The next day, the Feast of the Cross was kept in a way that had never been heard of before. The church-members formed in procession as for a funeral, some carrying the holy pictures, others bearing lighted candles and waving incense before them. They wended their way round the hills to the lonely "House of the Dead," the common village sepulcher used so generally in the mountains. The pictures were reverently carried in, placed against the walls with candles and incense before them, and there they were left with the dead. The procession then wound back to the emptied church, through which the fresh Lebanon breezes now blew as untrammeled as through a Puritan meeting-house. Some of the people were terror-stricken at what they had done, but the large number felt, though dimly, that somehow they stood more closely in the presence of the unseen God.

Presently there was a stir in the crowd and all made way for the aged but erect form of Abu Nameh, among them again for the first time in many weeks, his face glorified with a new joy. At that moment a ray of sunshine struck through the window above the door, covered until now by the largest of the gilded pictures. The ray touched the bared head of Abu Nameh and lingered like a blessing upon his white hair. To the people watching awe-struck it seemed a halo, and they realized that in place of their dead saints they had gained a living one.

XII

HID TREASURE

I

IT was one of the bleakest and steepest of Syrian hillsides, a jagged mass of rocks unvaried save at the summit, far overhead, where one solitary column of unhewn stones stood against the sky. It was piled there, probably, to frighten away jackals, but from what, it was difficult to say, as no sign of human abode or cultivation was to be seen.

Not unfitted to the wild surroundings was the hardy figure of a girl making her way boldly over the rocks. She was about fourteen, firmly built and erect, with the poise which only a mountain woman who has carried a jar on her head since childhood can gain. She stepped fearlessly, never touching the rocks with her hands as she climbed. Her attention was absorbed, as she searched for something among the crevices; there was a look of fierce determination in her black eyes.

"I know it is here," she repeated to herself; "it is only because I do not know the spell that I cannot find it."

She stopped before a large flat rock, in which were hewn oblong depressions, well squared at the corners, evidently ancient tombs.

"The trouble is, these have been emptied of their treasure long ago. But there must be others like them."

She screened her eyes from the sun and gazed around her, the wind blowing her tangled hair into her face, wrapping her coarse blue garments about her.

"Who is that?" she exclaimed, looking eagerly at a spot on the opposite slope. Plainly some one was there, and not a mountaineer.

"It is a foreigner!" exclaimed Lamyeh

again, trembling with excitement, "and he has a book! It will tell where the treasure is; that is what books are for, my father told me."

She hurried breathlessly down the hillside and up the other slope, this time keeping as much as possible behind the rocks. She reached a point a little above the stranger, where she could watch him unnoticed. She had never seen any one like him before, with light hair and fair skin, now rather burned by the sun, and such trig foreign garments, so plainly meant for use and quick motion, not a fold allowed for graceful effect. She noticed his dusty leggings, and concluded that he had come a long horseback journey. Something in his strongly cut features and even in his absorbed manner of reading and in his positive way of writing from time to time on a scrap of paper showed a man of determination.

"He is copying the directions," thought Lamyeh.

But what attracted her attention most was a small round object in a leather case strapped over his shoulder; she felt sure that this was the clock which would point out the right spot.

She grew impatient waiting. How could he sit so calmly when the secret was his? At last he folded his paper and shut his book upon it. Lamyeh clutched the sharp rock with excitement—he would start now! But no, he only changed his position, bending forward and covering his face with his hands. Lamyeh gazed with an unaccustomed sense of awe, and her black eyes fell in shame as though she had been profaning something.

She cowered behind the rock until he started down the valley, to her surprise, in the direction of the village in the bend below. She followed him, coming closer as he neared the limit of the rocks. He walked with a step as bold as hers. Presently, to her consternation, a couple of men appeared upon the path below. What could be more trying?

"They will see us and spoil it all."

With the bewildering sense that now was her last moment, she ran down the remaining distance like a hunted wild creature and greatly surprised the gentleman with her breathless greeting.

"Oh, please, for the sake of St. Elias, tell

me where the treasure is." There was something pathetic in her earnestness.

The stranger smiled—a frank, kindly smile.
He was not unacquainted with the beliefs cur-
rent in the region.

"You are mistaken," he said; "we foreigners
are not here to look for your gold; we do not
know where it is."

Lamyeh looked puzzled. "But your clock
will tell," she said, pointing to the instrument
in the leather case.

The young man laughed with a hearty
amusement that quite disconcerted her.

"This is what we call a barometer," he said,
opening the case; "it shows how high the mountains are and tells when it is going to rain."

Lamyeh's respect for him was fast diminish-
ing. "Why, we know that without a clock."

But by this time the men from the village
had reached them, and Lamyeh slunk back
under their looks of angry disapproval. They
greeted the stranger warmly.

"You have delayed a long time," said one.
"We have had to hold the road like robbers to
keep the village people from following you
up the rocks."

"Thank you," said the gentleman. "I suppose they hardly understand why I want time to prepare my sermon."

His host bowed respectfully, never showing by word or look his own doubts on the subject.

The other man, who happened to be Lamyeh's uncle, turned upon her with repressed indignation. "Be off with you, you dry-faced hussy. What impudence are you trying now, talking with the minister?"

Lamyeh fled back to her rocks and stood shading her eyes, watching the three disappear down the path.

"He does not mean to tell me, that's sure! Never mind, I'll find it in spite of him! He has no right; it is mine!"

She struck up the hill again to the spot where the stranger had been and sat down where he had sat, facing in the direction that he had faced. She could not help a furtive glance back toward the corner where she had hidden, as though dreading the intrusion of her own presence, but all was quiet. She opened her hands before her like a book and bent her restless black eyes upon them; then looked up, as the calm blue eyes had done before.

She stifled a cry and darted forward, bending upon her knees. Her eyes had not deceived her; there under the gray lichens, just above the level of the ground, was a seam in the rock. Tingling with excitement, she grubbed away the soil with her hands, and disclosed the outline of a slab. She could hardly control her joy as she pried it out and uncovered an open space behind. She could not see anything in the dark hole in this faint evening light, but with her hands she could feel the square-cut faces of the hollow, and she knew certainly that it was an ancient tomb. Then her hand struck something; she knew in a moment what it was! With madly beating heart she drew it out and shook it; it was a small jar, and something rattled in it. She turned it over confidently, certain of her success, and would have been surprised if she had not seen the glimmer of real gold. There were three coins, engraved with fair, classic heads, of far greater value than Lamyeh dreamed; sufficient for her that they were real gold, the first she had ever handled.

II

Lamyeh bounded down the hillside with a triumphant feeling in her heart which it was hard to conceal.

Fortunately for her, she found the family at home quite preoccupied with another subject. The younger children were full of the news:

"The Frangi gentleman has come from Ain-el-Hajar to preach here to-morrow, and he is going to open a school in the village!"

"I have seen him already, and have talked with him," said Lamyeh, with a superior air; but nothing more would she disclose.

The next day was a memorable one in the little village. The foreign gentleman had come from his central mission station in answer to a petition for a school from a delegation of the villagers.

"We will give the house," they said, "if you will send the teacher."

So, after the usual Sunday mass in the early morning, the people assembled in the room set apart for the new school and listened to a sermon the like of which they had never heard before—a story told in plain words, such as they used in their own homes, with a personal touch about it that brought a new meaning into their simple village lives.

But a far different impulse was at work just now upon Lamyeh, who waited until the people had all assembled at the service, then made her way hastily in the opposite direction.

It was only a few minutes' walk down the valley to the Sacred Tree under which the village saint was buried. The old oak, with low-spreading gnarled branches, a forlorn memorial of the forests which once clung to the sides of Lebanon, now stood alone in the desolate valley, its ragged patch of shade the only break in the glare of rocks. Now in its old age, with uncouth outline, it remained like an aged beggar by the roadside, whose dignity of years is shamed by garments of rags. For the limbs of the oak, seamed and wrinkled, showed now through fantastic streamers of rag —red, blue, brown—all faded and tattered, fluttering in the wind. It was the price of sanctity, for the tree was now a shrine, and from all the country round would come men and women bringing rags from the bedsides of their sick ones to tie to the twigs of the Holy

Tree, with a prayer to the saint buried beneath.

Lamyeh looked up at the fluttering tokens with a feeling of reverence. To her they meant the power ruling over human destinies.

"Each one of these is a prayer," she said to herself. "My treasure will be safe."

So she buried the precious coins at the roots of the tree, beside the saint's tomb, and went away with a sense of assured safety.

She took care to keep out of the missionary's sight; she would run no risk of having her secret disclosed.

She felt considerable relief when she heard, Monday morning, that he had gone. She could now enjoy the thought of her possessions undisturbed. While she fed her sheep in the yard, mechanically stuffing handfuls of mulberry leaves into its mouth, her mind danced with visions of bracelets, necklace, and a silk gown. The chickens hopped past her into the house to pick at the winter's store of wheat piled on the floor, and her baby brother cried and squirmed under the tight straps of his cradle, but Lamyeh noticed nothing.

"Does a girl named Lamyeh live here?" asked a sweet voice.

Lamyeh looked up, amazed, into a face that
seemed a part of her dream-world. A young
woman with fresh, clear complexion and delicate features, a pink-flowered veil thrown
lightly over her hair, stood in the path, a crock
of milk in her hand.

Lamyeh rose in confusion, pushing back
her tangled locks from her eyes and wiping her
hands on her dress.

"If this is Lamyeh," said the sweet voice
again, "I have come to ask you a favor. I am
your new neighbor, the school-teacher's wife.
I want to make curds as you make them here,
and they say you are famous in that line and
will show me how."

Lamyeh's face glowed with gratification and
returning self-respect.

"Come in, please," she urged with a gra-
ciousness quite new to her wild nature, reaching down a chair from its nail on the wall. "I
thought my mother went to see you this morning."

"Yes, indeed," said the visitor, "and she
helped me beautifully to get my house in order.
With her permission I come to you now."

Lamyeh looked delighted. From a niche

in the mud wall she brought a bit of white powder which she put into her visitor's palm.

"You make a paste of that with a little milk," she explained, "and then stir it into the crock."

The guest held the powder in her hand and looked at Lamyeh as though waiting for something.

"Well, don't you want to do it?" asked Lamyeh.

The visitor, in her turn, became embarrassed.

"I thought you meant to bring a cup or something to mix it in."

"Oh, no," said Lamyeh, "we mix it in the palm of the hand."

"Oh!" said the stranger, enlightened, but still looking helplessly at the crock of milk; "then may I trouble you for a spoon to dip it out with?"

Lamyeh laughed outright. "Why, we do that with our fingers." The city lady seemed remarkably prejudiced in her ideas.

Her guest flushed. "If I am to put my fingers in I would like to wash them first; may I have some water?"

This was too much for Lamyeh. "Why, of

course we wash our hands, but we do that after-wards."

When the lesson was completed and the visitor was taking her leave, Lamyeh caught her hand with a look of appeal.

"What would you like?" said the sweet-faced lady.

"Please," said Lamyeh, "can you tell me of any medicine for removing freckles?"

III

The friendship thus begun soon became to Lamyeh an absorbing passion. The teacher's wife, Sitt Lulu they called her, a mountain girl herself, became Lamyeh's ideal. "You are my saint," she would say; "I would light my ten fingers as candles before you."

Little could Lamyeh realize the sacrifice that it meant for Lulu Yusuf and her husband, products of a new order of things, to come back, with their larger aspirations and refined tastes, to this primitive village life. What Lamyeh did realize was a new interest in her own mind in things that she had never cared for before. The first step was an appreciation of the use and value of a comb. Other things

followed rapidly. Before long her roving black
eyes were studying eagerly what had once been
to her only a symbol of the supernatural—a
book. And with the new growth in self-respect
was always the underlying satisfaction—Lamyeh's secret—that she, the mountain girl, was
an heiress!

Lamyeh spent much time lingering about
the sacred Rag Tree, dreaming of the time
when she should unearth her treasures. Once
she dug up the coins to make sure that they
were safe, but put them back, judging rightly
that even if they were found no one would
dare desecrate the place by taking them.

One spring day, when the snows of the
upper Lebanon were melting, sending many
streams down among the barren rocks, Lamyeh went again to visit her tree. Before long
the sound of thunder rolled in from the distant
mountains.

The roar repeated itself surprisingly soon,
echoing across the nearer rocks. Before
long the sky was black. Lamyeh gazed
in wonder; she had never seen storm-clouds
gather so fast. Then came the first drops,
large and far apart, and Lamyeh started to

hurry home. But before she had run many steps the rain was pouring hard, and she turned back to the tree for shelter. She realized soon that this was a mistake, and that the ever-increasing storm was something unusual. But it was too late now to fight her way home; the mountainsides seemed a torrent.

An hour or so passed, and then came a terrible roar, with crashing and grinding of rocks, from the direction of the village above. Lamyeh had barely time to swing herself up into the tree before the flood was rushing past, carrying stones and trees before it. Then, to Lamyeh's horror, beams, pieces of woodwork and broken furniture were swept by, and her heart sickened at the thought of her own home at the bottom of the village, in the very path of the torrent. But all she could do was to hold on desperately, while the water swirled below her and the great tree creaked and groaned like a ship at sea, and above her head the fantastic rag streamers fluttered and flapped in a wild mockery of glee.

It was hours before Lamyeh could struggle back over the rocks to the village. And what a scene she beheld! All the lower row of houses gone, her own home with the rest. The village people were gathered about the ruins, with much crying and wringing of hands.

Lamyeh was greeted like one returning from death. Her mother threw herself on her neck in a transport of grateful tears.

"Thank God! thank God! we are all safe now; never mind about the house."

The sudden "seil" or flood, so much dreaded in some parts of Lebanon, had undermined the terraces in the upper section of the village, carrying down an avalanche of rocks and soil upon the homes in the lower section with all their scanty furnishings and the precious store of wheat—the family provision. No wonder the people wept. But they bore their losses with the resignation which is the strength of the Oriental nature. As Lamyeh's mother said, "Can we build a tent above our heads to ward off the blows of God?"

Mercifully, no lives had been lost. Lamyeh had now but one thought: "I can now give bread to my family."

She could hardly wait till the next morning to go for her treasure. She stole out of her uncle's house, where they had been taken in

for the present, before any of the rest were
awake. She reached the Sacred Tree breathless; but oh, what a change was there! The
soil below had been washed away in great
masses, and the bared roots now grasped helplessly at the empty air. Not a sign of even
the place where the treasure had been! Lamyeh stood stunned in bitterness of wo, such as
she had never known in her life.

With a sob of despair she turned to leave the
hateful spot, when her eye fell on something
caught among the roots. She picked it up and
saw that it was a book, washed down, no doubt,
from the village. It was wet and covered with
mud, but she wiped it off as well as she could
and opened it to see what it was. And the
words that she read were these: "The king-
dom of heaven is like unto a treasure hidden
in the field which a man found and hid; and in
his joy he goeth and selleth all that he hath,
and buyeth that field."

The words struck into Lamyeh's very soul.
"All that he hath! all that he hath!" Who, if
not Lamyeh, could know what that meant?

"O God!" she cried, "what can make up
for all that one hath?"

In her distress she thought instinctively of her friend Lulu. "She can tell me if anybody in the world can." And she went to her at once, with her own impetuous frankness.

In the middle of the morning Lamyeh returned to her mother with a radiance in her black eyes which glorified her whole face. Her mother looked at her amazed; she had never thought Lamyeh beautiful before.

"Mother," she said, "I have found hid treasure."

XIII

NIMR'S KUSSIS

THE great peak of Hermon rose grim
and solitary over a scene of sunset
glory. At its feet lay the whole land
of Syria, like a picture in relief, its parallel
chains of mountains mere seams upon the landscape.

Rufail Haddad, alone upon the bleak summit, looked down upon the scene as on a world
apart from himself, whose pettiness no longer
appealed to him. His face was turned to the
west, where stretched the great sea, covered
now by a still more wondrous ocean of cloud,
which rolled billow after billow to the horizon.

The sunset rays streamed over the vast expanse, in burning tints of red and gold. "A sea of glass mingled with fire," murmured Rufail to himself.

The cloud-billows rolled on till they touched the peaks of Lebanon, pouring over them like a cataract; but here a marvelous change took place. The hot dry air rising from the Bakaa plain met the overflowing cataract and dissipated it, and the torrent rolled into nothingness.

Rufail followed the sweep of the horizon, past the faint green patches that marked the sites of Damascus and far distant desert towns, to the great eastern plain, stretching in opal tints, with its extinct volcanic craters outlined against their own black shadows like mountains that one sees upon the surface of the moon. Across the plain stretched a black mysterious shape, strangely clear in its conical form, the shadow of Hermon itself. Rufail watched it as it lengthened, drawing into its grasp more and more of the plain, till it reached the eastern horizon; then like a living creature it leaped into the sky, ever rising, dark and ominous against the clouds, till it was absorbed at last into the surrounding darkness.

Rufail leaned forward upon his hand, so intent on the scene that he did not notice until they were close upon him the figures of three armed men approaching him from three directions. In an instant his dreamy look was gone, and his quick glance upon the intruders told that their object was understood. He picked up three stone chips from the disintegrated rock at his feet, and looked meaningly from one to another of the three men; next he placed the chips upon a rock about fifteen paces away, then, stepping back to his first position, lifted his revolver, and without taking appreciable time to aim, blew the chips to pieces in quick succession.

"Mashallah!" exclaimed the head-brigand, admiringly, "your aim is like the eagle's glance."

Rufail could now halloo to his companion, who, hearing the shots, was hastening toward him from the snow-drift below, but before he reached the summit the three robbers had slipped away.

The two young men looked at each other

with a sober sense of their own recklessness.

"I suppose you were right," said Rufail; "it was foolish to come alone."

"Oh, no," laughed his friend, a little nervously, "I was the fool; I see now it takes a 'kus'* to beat a robber."

They walked back together to their campfire and passed a peaceful night in the old high place of Baal, the "Cave of the Winds." The next day was spent in hunting, as they had planned, and in the afternoon they started down again to their homes. They separated at the valley road, each turning toward his own village.

With the familiar path Rufail found himself again resuming the cares and responsibilities of his difficult life. Five years ago he had met the question that must be answered in these days by every young Syrian of Christian education. Should he leave once for all his old depressing surroundings of fixed custom, throw himself into the wide-awake life of America, with its mental stimulus, its promises and rewards—should not he, too, one among the many, have a chance to rise in the world?

* Kus, or kussis, is the Arabic word for pastor.

Or, on the other hand, should he remain where his high ideals might be poorly understood, among a people held down by ignorance and adverse conditions, whose advancement must be gained by infinite patience, yet whose advancement he might help? A question something like this was decided by Moses long ago upon the banks of the Nile. The decision with Rufail had resulted in his coming to an obscure mountain village as kussis over a small mission church, with a congregation of rough peasants, and a salary of most humble dimensions.

Rufail turned the bend that led to his home and was met by the sight of the village in flames! He saw at once what had happened; the unfriendly village across the valley had thus wreaked its spite. He hurried on in wretched self-condemnation for leaving his people for even one holiday. Presently he was met by a group of horsemen.

"*Ishlah!* Disarm!" they cried.

There was no use resisting. Rufail gave up his arms and what little money he carried.

"Now walk ahead of us," ordered one.

Rufail saw that he must obey and started

back on his path, steep rocks on one side, a precipice on the other. He walked half a mile, often looking back to see what his captors were about. Suddenly he saw them aim their guns at him. There was not a moment to lose; he leaped the precipice and fell heavily upon the ground below. The horsemen rode up quickly and looked down.

"He is dead," said one; "we need not waste fire upon him."

They rode on, while Rufail became conscious of his injuries. There was a sharp pain in his side, another in his leg which he could not move; then he lost himself again.

He woke up to find a rough face bending over him, full of anxiety; he had seen the face before, though he could not remember where.

"A lad who can shoot like you will not be left to die while Nimr has breath," said the rough man kindly.

Rufail recognized him now as the robber chief who had threatened him on Hermon.

"I am going to carry you to your home," said Nimr. "The pillagers have left the town."

He lifted Rufail upon his back. Every

motion caused the injured man agony, but he did not show it. The long climb was accomplished with much difficulty and suffering to both, and the smoldering village, now seemingly deserted, was reached.

The enemy had set fire to the booths of leaves which formed the entrance to most of the houses, and these had communicated the fire to the roofs; the stone and mud walls remained, blackened and bare.

With almost despairing hope, Rufail directed his bearer to his own house, only to find it in ruins like the rest. But the church which adjoined it, with its tiled roof, stood uninjured. Its door was locked, as usual.

"Would you hunt under the embers of my house for the keys?" asked Rufail.

"Shame on my beard if I cannot do that!" answered the robber, laying him down.

Rufail directed him where to look, and, without shrinking, the man stepped among the burning ruins. He returned soon with the three great keys. He threw them down quickly, rubbing his hands on the earth. Rufail could see, even in the faint light, that both hands and feet were severely burned.

"The Lord reward you," he murmured.

When the keys were cool enough to handle, Nimr tried the lock with one after another, without success; the heat had warped them out of shape.

"You will have to break down the door," said Rufail, wearily.

"And leave the way open for your enemies? Never, by my girdle!"

He again took up the first key that he had tried. Raising it solemnly before him, he repeated, "Bism Illah! In the name of God!" then fitted it into the keyhole.

The door opened! The church was a simple stone room, fitted with rude benches and pulpit. Nimr groped his way in, spread his own goat's-hair coat upon the floor for a bed, and carefully laid Rufail upon it, lifting the young man's head upon his own lap for a pillow. In spite of all Rufail's entreaties, that he should take some rest himself, he sat up with Rufail thus the whole night.

In the early morning, the villagers began creeping back to their ruined homes. It became noised about that the kussis was lying wounded in the church, and Rufail was soon surrounded by sympathetic friends, all anxious to do him service.

"What he needs is a doctor," said one, "but who of us would dare go over the mountains for him at this time, with our enemies hunting the high-roads for us?"

"I will go," said Nimr; "no one will dare touch me. I will have the doctor here before night." Then a quizzical look came over his face. "I suppose the doctor will not trust himself to me; you had better give me a paper."

Rufail scratched off a few lines with difficulty. Nimr folded the paper into a tight roll and slipped it into the hollow of his reed cane. He smiled for the first time.

"They may search me now if they like, they will never guess my errand."

He was gone all day, while the people gave Rufail the best of what little remained to them. By night the Syrian doctor arrived, with his strange brigand guide. He was an old friend of Rufail's; not many years before, they had studied together in the school at Sidon. The broken leg was set and the bruised limbs made more comfortable, then came the inevitable treatment of a multitude of ailments that suddenly manifest themselves in a crowd at the appearance of a doctor. He left the next morning with the blessings of the village upon his head.

During the long convalescence which followed Nimr would never leave his patient. When fever was upon Rufail, he would bathe his head, and with gruff insistence would keep away the ever-solicitous crowd of friends. Sometimes he would sit, with Rufail's head again upon his lap, gazing with awe upon the painted letters on the wall.

"What do they mean?" he asked, one day. Rufail read them aloud—the Lord's Prayer and the Ten Commandments.

"Is that your religion?" asked Nimr.

"It is the key to it," answered Rufail.

"W'Allah! it is a strange doctrine," said the robber. "The Bedouins, who brought me up, taught me that the noblest aim in the world was to kill and rob and swear by God's name, and never to forgive a trespass."

Rufail turned and raised himself upon his elbow in his earnestness. "Nimr, have you nothing to be forgiven?"

From that time till Rufail recovered he used

to read daily to Nimr from the great Bible, which lay on the pulpit, doctrines at first distasteful and incomprehensible to the hardened robber, explaining them till they became to him at first familiar, and finally beautiful.

The bright day came for Rufail's return to the house which had been rebuilt for him. But to Nimr the day brought only the deepest gloom. Before light, he rose from his mat at Rufail's side and bent over him with a father's tenderness, kissing him first on one cheek, then on the other, without a word. An hour later, when the joyous people met, Nimr was gone.

He was seldom seen again among the villagers, but it became a well-known fact that he robbed no more. Hunting or carrying messages through dangerous parts of the country became his chief employment. Several times a year the dark man would suddenly appear among Rufail's little congregation. Seating himself upon the floor cross-legged, with folded arms, he would listen with face intent upon the young preacher; when the service was over he would go, often without a word.

If ever it happened that any of Rufail's people were robbed by other brigands upon the

high-roads, word had but to be sent to Nimr
and the goods were always restored.

As for Rufail himself, no man of rank in
the region could as safely go and come as he,
however wild the district; for among brigands
and villagers alike he was known and honored
as Nimr's kussis.

WHERE EAST AND WEST MEET

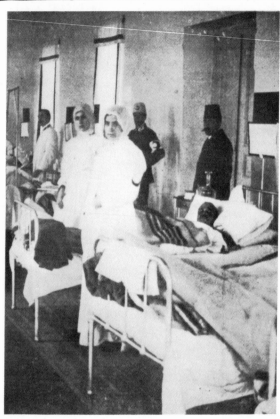

Military Hospital

XIV

THE NIGHT
AT IBIL

SOMETHING new was happening in the little inland village of Ibil, nestled near the flanks of Mt. Hermon, and most of the inhabitants turned out to see. Five stocky traveling horses jogged wearily into town with the dust of two days' journey covering them and their riders.

"Why, they're three mere girls!" exclaimed old Im Asaad. "How could their parents in America let them come so far?"

"That's their Arabic teacher, the Syrian lady on the front horse, and the boy is their cook,—looks as if he didn't know which end of a spoon to hold."

They were greeted with whole-souled cor-

191

diality by the Syrian Protestant pastor and his wife and an eager group of village church-members. They were escorted by the whole bevy to the little house which they had hired for the summer, four rooms with mud walls and floors, but homelike withal.

"Look at this ladder leading up to our roof!" exclaimed Helen. They all gleefully climbed it, and took a survey of their surroundings.

"We shall have company in our loneliness," said Lois. "I have been counting the inhabitants of our front yard. We have three horses, two mules, a cow, a donkey, three sheep, two broods of chickens and all the neighbors' children, right at our door-step!"

The girl-missionaries were soon settled in their simple housekeeping, with cots and camp-stools, while the servant-boy, Shahin, managed the cooking over an earthen grate on the floor of a mud hut across the yard.

Their opportunities for learning Arabic soon exceeded their wildest hopes, and visitors from seven in the morning till bedtime became the order of the day.

At first the girls made it a rule to speak

Arabic together at meals, but Helen finally protested.

"We cannot possibly get the nourishment of our food if we rack our brains all the meal-hour trying to remember the word for 'hash'!"

But the Arabic progressed rapidly in other ways, and at the end of a month the girls felt justified in taking a two-days' vacation. Grammars were closed and Miss Asma was prevailed upon to make a well-earned visit to her own home. The girls waved her a good-by from the flat roof as she rode away, her little donkey-boy scampering along behind.

With the last glimpse, the girls turned to each other, a little ripple of excitement in the look which they exchanged.

"We shall test our pluck now," said Helen, "and see what it is like to be alone in the village."

They celebrated their holiday by an excursion with the pastor to a neighboring town of historic interest. There, under the imposing shadow of Hermon, had occurred many years before one of the most harrowing events on record, when a thousand Christian men, women, and children, were decoyed into the castle and slaughtered like sheep. The girls passed with horror through the dreary vaults, saw the hole in the floor where the blood had flowed out, and gazed awestruck at the time-stained walls, wondering what untold mysteries they might reveal. They rode home at sunset, their excited imaginations in such tension that every black shadow among the rocks seemed vested with a nameless dread. They tried to throw it off, talking gaily together, but the thoughts awakened were too solemn to be treated lightly. It was not so much the recollection of a past event that stirred them, but the realization that these self-same deeds were being repeated in regions akin to this.

"How incapable we are of imagining anything until it comes personally before us," reflected Helen.

They were now back at their own door-step and had to say good-by to their kind friend the pastor.

But the evening passed without incident and at night the three cots were as comfortable as usual with their undulations and cavities, and the girls were soon deep in "the dreamless sleep of youth."

It was after midnight when all three were roused by something unearthly; it took several minutes for their confused consciousness to realize what it was. It seemed to be outside of their windows, a wild babel, women's screams and men's shouts, all alive with the unmistakable tone of terror and distress.

"What is it?" whispered Lois.

"It may be wailing for the dead," said Fulda, "but I never heard it so terrible as this; some one must have been killed."

She slipped to the window and looked out; in the pale moonlight she could see excited groups of men and women, shrieking and throwing their arms frantically in the air as they hurried up the hillside in a panic.

"What do you think of bolting the windows?" she suggested.

The girls were not slow to respond to the idea and in an incredibly short time bolts that had never worked before were slipped into place.

All the time, the horrid sounds were dinning in their ears.

"Shall we call Shahin?" asked Lois.

"*You* may, if you like," answered Helen,

"you have to go out-of-doors to reach his room."

Lois grew thoughtful. "I doubt if he could help us," she reflected meekly. They listened in the darkness as the sounds became louder and wilder.

"Oh, wo is me! wo is me!" shrieked a woman's voice, in agony.

It was lost in a thundering bass: "Your house be destroyed! Your life be cut off!"

Then rose the mountaineers' war-cry, followed by more shrieks, which burst out, and then seemed to be stifled and choked, as though the victims were being trampled down; then came the thud of many feet.

"O Lord, save us!" came the cry.

The girls recalled now all too well references they had heard to a standing feud between the two factions of the village, and the awful issue became evident.

"Suppose we barricade the door," suggested Helen. "Do you think we could lift our heavy wooden chests?"

They managed it somehow, stumbling across the room in the darkness, and piled the boxes one above another against the door.

"I never supposed we were so strong," panted Fulda.

They sat down again in a row on the edge of the cot; nothing would have tempted them to strike a light.

"It seems to me I hear a wounded man calling for water," whispered Lois. "I wonder if we ought to give the injured people refuge in our house."

"I hardly see how we could," answered Helen; "we do not know who are the victims, and who are the enemies."

"Fulda," said Lois, "if they *should* break in on us, couldn't you speak to them, say something that might soften their hearts? You were born and brought up in this country."

"Yes, I have been thinking about it," answered Fulda. "I thought I might remind them that my father is a doctor and has spent his life treating their people and ask them, if they should ever be wounded and need to go to him, if they would not be sorry for having killed his daughter."

"I should think that ought to appeal to them," said Lois.

"Girls," said Helen, "I think we ought to

dress in our warmest clothes and be ready to escape over the mountains if necessary."

The girls followed the suggestion promptly, gathering together their wraps with hurried fingers, while the mind of each called up in anxious succession every rock and turn of the road that led to the nearest mission station.

"I would rather trust to our friends here," said Lois. "I know the pastor would risk his last chance of life to save us."

"Indeed he would," answered Helen warmly, "if—if he is still here to do it."

"There's his voice," exclaimed Lois.

It rose strong and clear, "Young men! Come this way! All work together!" then it was drowned in the clamor.

They listened in silence as the tumult went on, perhaps two hours.

It was an experience which will help them as long as life lasts, that quiet waiting in the darkness with the fiendish sounds in their ears and the prospect of death so close. Each confessed afterward that she prepared her mind during those hours for the particular death that seemed to her most probable; Helen expected to be shot, Fulda to be stabbed, while

brave little Lois steeled her heart at the prospect of having her throat cut. But, to their
credit be it said, they were perfectly calm
throughout. Indeed, death face to face seemed
not so strange after all, and as the three
girls kneeled together beside the cot, they felt
sincerely that they could face whatever might
come.

At last the tumult wore away; the people
seemed to disperse and silence fell, more mysterious and awful even than the uproar. A
strange sense of surprise crept over the girls
as they realized that they might live after all;
in that moment life appeared like a new and
untried experience; indeed, it seemed as solemn
to live as to die.

When the dawn began to break through the
cracks of the windows, the girls ventured to
take down their barricade and open the door.
The light was gray and uncertain and the
cool air felt strange upon their heated faces,
but there was nothing unusual in the little yard.
An old woman, the landlord's mother, was sitting on the door-step feeding her sheep with
mulberry-leaves. Fulda went out and spoke
to her.

"What has happened?" she asked breathlessly. "Tell me how many were killed?"

The old woman looked at her curiously, then lifted up her mulberry-stained hands and laughed a long quavering laugh.

"What do you mean?" repeated Fulda.

The woman answered with a voluble story in Arabic, Fulda listening with a growing expression of amusement on her face.

She turned back to the room.

"What did she say?" asked Lois eagerly; "we could not hear."

"Such a climax!" exclaimed Fulda. "Do you remember Abu Milhem's little half-underground store-room, that was so closely packed with chopped straw? Well, some one went in there last night with a lamp and accidentally set the place on fire. It did not blaze up, but just smoldered under the earthen roof. But you know a fire is such an unheard-of thing in these mud and stone villages, that the people completely lost head over it. The whole population rushed pell-mell to the place, fairly running over each other in their excitement. There was hardly any water in the houses about and you remember the fountain is a mile away, so they tried to stamp the fire out with their feet, but of course they were in each other's way and of course they grew angry and screamed and cursed at each other and some of them became frightened and pandemonium was the result. All over a smoldering hut!"

"And we went through all the horror and solemnity of being massacred just for that!" exclaimed Helen.

"Yes, just for that."

XV

LUCIYEH OF
THE BRAVE
HEART *

A DIPLOMA! Luciyeh's cheeks were flushed and her brown eyes scanned eagerly the seal of the Syrian Protestant college, her alma mater, with its emblem the wide-spreading cedar of Lebanon. She was alone in her room now, where she had lived these happy, busy years of her nurse's training-course. The excitement of commencement was over, her roommate had returned already to her own home in Nazareth, and Luciyeh would leave in a few days. What a proud, glad home-coming it would be, with the welcome that she had earned! Her mind pictured again the horror on her mother's face when she first proposed taking the nurse's training-

---

* An incident of the late Italian war.

course in the city. It was in their simple but cheerful home on Mt. Lebanon; through the open doorway was wafted the spring scent of blossoming broom-shrubs, which made the hillside a flame of gold.

"You turn everything upside down with your foreign ideas!" said her mother, bitterly. "Here is Elias, the widower, asking for you, and not even objecting to your being twenty-five years old!"

Luciyeh's face deeply flushed now at the recollection of her resentment at her mother's words.

"Elias wants only some one to care for his eight children. I am nothing to him, and he is certainly nothing to me." She held back from further comment with the self-control that she had learned through years of mission-school training.

"Oh, my two eyes, my mother! I have worked for you and earned money for you, and taken care of my dear father through years of illness, and now my little sister is through with school and is ready to take my place at home. You do not need me, and there are many sick and helpless who do."

The mother yielded unwillingly, and Luci-yeh came to the new, beautifully equipped training-school in the city by the sea. She met with hard work for brain and body, but she greeted both with the enthusiasm which filled her life with gladness.

Then came that vacation at home. According to their old habit in the festive days of ripe grapes, the family rose at dawn and carried bread, olives, and fresh village cheese to supplement the royal breakfast that awaited them in their vineyard outside the village. There they could pick wondrous clusters of dew-covered black grapes, large as young plums; bunches of "hens-and-chickens," large grapes with little ones hanging round them; delicate "lady's fingers," slender white grapes two inches long; pink-bloomed "maiden's cheeks," that reflected Luciyeh's own color; but as satisfactory as any, the every-day little white grapes, that the poorest in the land could enjoy unstinted. The Syrian family is hampered by no limits when it is a question of grapes picked from the vines.

All were gay, till a sudden cry and a crackling of branches revealed the dear mother

fallen from a terrace in trying to reach an overhanging cluster. All ran to her rescue, but
their efforts to raise her produced agony.
Luciyeh was on her knees, feeling the injured
thigh with tender and skilful fingers.

"Dear, dear mother!—this is a compound
fracture," and she hastily sent her little brother
back to the house for her antiseptics and bandages.

News of the mishap traveled like wildfire to
the neighboring vineyards, and friends rapidly
collected with kindly advice.

"Kill a sheep and wrap the warm skin over
the wound," cried one.

"Yes," answered Luciyeh scornfully, "and
give her lockjaw from infection."

"I will get you a plaster from the barnyard,"
said another.

His wisdom was checked by a breathless ap-
parition, a bent and tottering old dame, tooth-
less, but with piercing eyes gleaming through
matted locks of gray hair, unevenly dyed with
red. In her hand she carried a basket covered
over with grape-leaves.

"I am the bone-setter of the village over the
hill. I am the only one who knows what to do.

In the Holy Name, make way!" She opened her basket, took out an earthen bowl, which covered a quantity of eggs.

"There are twenty," she said, proceeding to break one and separate the whites into the bowl. "All these will stiffen the bandage finely. Take this veil of mine," she went on, handing the dirty object to Luciyeh, "and tear it into shreds." Luciyeh, who had been struck dumb by a distracted instinct to show reverence for old age, suddenly found her voice.

"Grandmother," she said, with an effort at respect in her tone, "better to bind her with chains to her bed for the rest of her life. If we put this stiff bandage on now, the limb will swell beneath it and gangrene will follow."

"You she-ass, do you presume to instruct *me?*" The piercing eyes shot fire, and, pushing Luciyeh aside, the scrawny hands seized the lacerated wound. The sufferer gave a scream and the wound began to pour red blood.

"She has broken an artery!" exclaimed Luciyeh, white with indignation. "Take that woman away," she commanded, like a little queen. Several young men found themselves obeying. On her knees, Luciyeh was quickly and deftly at work. A piece of cord from the grape basket, a stick picked up from the ground, and in a few minutes the admiring group beheld a tourniquet tightly applied, the hemorrhage stopped.

"Bravo! Bravo!" cried all.

By this time the little brother was back with the antiseptic tablets and dressings. A clean bandage was soon in place, and under the directions of the little commanding officer, the mother was placed upon an improvised stretcher.

"We must go right to the city and have the fracture examined with the X-ray at the college."

By this time, not a question was raised. Two squads of young men agreed to take turns carrying the stretcher, while Luciyeh walked the entire fifteen miles of dusty white carriage-road beside her mother.

Great was the surprise of the hospital staff to see Luciyeh back again, but the doctors soon found reason to commend her skill and promptness. The X-rays were invoked, the surgeon's ability called forth, and at last the exhausted mother was laid in a restful bed in her daughter's ward.

During the weeks which followed, the invisible knitting of the bones and the healing of torn tissue was no more miraculous than the gradual growth in the mother's heart of appreciation of Luciyeh's work. Not only were her own sore muscles soothed by her daughter's invigorating touch, but with tear-filled eyes she watched Luciyeh moving from bed to bed, noted how pain-drawn faces relaxed after her ministrations, and discouraged eyes brightened with life and hope from her cheery presence. When at last the mother went home, walking as erect as when a village child she first balanced a water-jar on her head, she carried in her bosom a great pride that it was her daughter who was rendering to her people such a service.

"And now I will take my diploma to my mother," murmured Luciyeh to herself, "to get her blessing."

There was a tap at the door. Luciyeh rose and her face grew radiant when she saw the tall, black-gowned figure and serene face which had grown to be her ideal during these three years. Mrs. Fitz-Gerald, widow of as devoted

a missionary as ever rode among the mountains and gorges of Lebanon, carried in her
calm face, not old, despite the snowy hair above
it, the sweetness that has come through pain.
As superintendent of the hospital she not only
brought the message of Jesus to the patients,
but she inspired in the young girls who worked
under her, a desire to carry the message too.

"I have a call for you," said Mrs. Fitz-
Gerald. "The governor of the city came to
me after the commencement exercises, asking
me to recommend a head nurse for the new hospital that the government is to establish. I
have recommended you."

The blood fled from Luciyeh's face. "How
could I do it? The only woman among all
those Moslem officials!"

"I believe you are called for such a time
as this," said Mrs. Fitz-Gerald.

"Will you help me?" asked Luciyeh.

"Indeed I will, and a Greater than I," replied her friend.

After a short visit home Luciyeh started in
earnest with her work. The officials showed
remarkable readiness to consider her rec-
ommendations and fulfil her requirements as

far as means would allow. The new building, on the edge of a dreary waste of sand at one side of the city, was fortunately empty. Luciyeh fairly quivered with excitement when the new equipment arrived, plain beds and material for bedding.

"We'll make up the bedding ourselves," she said.

Then there were cooking appliances and the sterilizer from her own hospital, which had been discarded when a splendid new one was sent by a generous giver in America. And of course there were medicines and a simple surgical outfit.

Luciyeh would not let Mrs. Fitz-Gerald come to see her till all was arranged and patients were admitted. Then, with a beating heart and pardonable pride, she took her teacher through the building.

"You see I have made everything as much as possible like things in my mother hospital. You recognize this arrangement of bedding and blankets and the way we prepare the patients' food?"

"Are these sick soldiers?" asked Mrs. Fitz-Gerald, entering a room where four soldiers in uniform were seated on a mat, smoking argilehs.

"Oh, no!" answered Luciyeh. "Sick prisoners are always sent here, and these soldiers are on guard to keep them from running away."

They had now reached the outer door.

"I only wish we had a wall around the premises. I don't feel very safe on the edge of the sands; vagabonds so often wander here; and every house in the city has a garden wall;— but that will come!" she broke off with characteristic brightness. "They say I am terrible, calling for expenditures!" They stepped outside together on the sand, so unlike the blossoming garden of the home hospital. Luciyeh took hold of both of Mrs. Fitz-Gerald's hands.

"Let me tell you one more thing I am going to have after the ways of our mother hospital. You always have daily prayers with the patients, and I am going to do the same." She bent her head over her teacher's hands and kissed them with the reverence she had learned when kissing her parents' hands as a little child.

"I learned it all from you," she said. Mrs. Fitz-Gerald returned the kiss on Luciyeh's forehead and both glowing cheeks.

"God bless you!" she whispered, and left, turning for a last glimpse of the sturdy little figure in white cap and uniform, unrelieved by beauty of surroundings, but giving out from her own personality an inspiring sense of energy, health, and helpfulness.

The months that followed seemed too short for the fulfilment of all Luciyeh's plans. Spring stole upon her unawares, with the warmer breezes of late February.

She stood at her window one early morning, gazing across the palm-tufted city to the snow-peaks of Lebanon, gloriously reflected in the glittering bay.

"There will be more patients," she mused, "as the spring travel grows easier. I will send to the mountains for my little cousin to come and work with me, and I will give her the nurse's training-course myself!"

Suddenly her eyes were riveted upon two vessels steaming swiftly toward the harbor. No new sight they were; war-ships of all nations frequented the busy seaport and exchange of salutes was as common as the decorous salaams of turbaned dignitaries on the streets. But there was something menacing in

the silently sliding gray monsters, not white
like pleasure-boats, nor black like the merchant
marine. The two battle-ships steamed more
rapidly and closer to shore than the usual visit-
ing squadrons, and immense flags were spread
amidships. Luciyeh brought her precious field-
glass to look. Her heart stood still: they were
Italian flags! The horrid war with Italy had
been going on for months, and dire news came
from a distance starting waves of apprehension in the city; but news from afar does not
stir for long. Now, suddenly, what could it
be? Perhaps a blockade, perhaps——

A tongue of fire shot from the forward ves-
sel and a screaming, hideous thing was hurled
directly across the city, over Luciyeh's head,
landing in the sand just beyond the hospital.
A second shell followed immediately, spanning
the city in another direction. Luciyeh flew
down-stairs to her people. Panic reigned.
Patients were scrambling out of bed, throwing
blankets about them, and rushing away from
the building.

"Stop! Stop!" she cried; but as well might
she have stopped the on-rushing shells. She
ran for the assistance of the soldiers, but they

had disappeared, and the prisoners had lost no time in escaping.

"The servants!" she panted, running to the kitchen, but they too were gone. In an incredibly short time Luciyeh found herself alone in her empty hospital. In the meantime, a new sound greeted her from the city, the sound never forgotten when once heard, the roar of an angry mob. She learned later what happened, a rush of the street-rabble to the barracks to seize arms for the defense of the city, —so they claimed. All she saw, away down in the streets, was a madly running horde, all with rifles, pointing in every direction. Several times she heard single shots and she knew well what that meant; some personal grudge scored off, a prostrate form lying in its blood, every one on the street running from the sight. She knew only too well the force of the rabble, the uncontrolled power of religious hate. Was a massacre beginning already? The hospital wall was still unbuilt!

The college clock struck nine. A few minutes more and there burst from the two battleships a volcano of horror, beggaring to insignificance the ordinary roll of powder salutes.

There was the sharp, crashing explosion of shells that hit—Oh, what were they striking? She remembered the two small Turkish gunboats which had been hiding in the harbor all winter; of course they were the targets. After a rain of fire a thing like a sea-serpent flew through the water, touching the larger gunboat. Instantly, a geyser arose and the gunboat had disappeared. The dull roar in the streets grew angrier and came nearer.

With one imploring look heavenward, Luciyeh ran from the deserted building, ran ever faster through the cactus-bordered lanes, back to her mother hospital. There overhead floated the symbol of safety, the American stars and stripes. Oh, beautiful vision—protection, assurance, peace! Many of the terrified neighbors, expecting a landing by the enemy with atrocities of all kinds, had run to the hospital for the shelter of the flag, and there was welcome for all.

Luciyeh ran through the excited group of nurses to her patron saint, Mrs. Fitz-Gerald, and sank down before her in sobs.

"What shall I do?" she gasped. The kind eyes that had watched her through her course looked tenderly down upon her, and the hand that had helped her so often was laid upon her shoulder.

"Luciyeh, go back to your work!" Luciyeh looked up, startled; could she mean such a cruel command? But the kind eyes did not falter. The girl clung to her passionately till her sobs were quiet, and all the while the brooding presence yearned over her, but did not speak. At last Luciyeh rose.

"I am going back," she said quietly.

"I knew you would," replied her guardian. "God will go with you."

Back through the questioning circle of nurses, back through the crowd of frightened neighbors, away from the protecting flag, down the steps she hurried, ever hastening lest her courage should give out. Back she fled through the menacing cactus-hedges, whose thorns pointed in every direction, like the guns of the mob down town.

"O God, make me strong, for Christ's sake!" she panted. Crossing a strip of open sand, she reached her deserted hospital, almost surprised to find it still there. She bolted the door after her and made a tour of inspection to assure

herself that no one was there. She was proceeding to put in order her dismantled wards,
when her heart stood still at a thundering
knock at the front door. She ran upstairs and
looked down through the window to see who
was there.

"For God's sake, open! Here is a wounded
man from the port."

Fear was gone. Here was some one to be
helped. She flew down, unbolted the door, and
the miserable sufferer was brought into the
operating-room. Jagged fragments of shell,
with horrid spiral motion, had done their worst
with soft human flesh. She wrung her hands.

"If only the hospital doctors were here!
They have not appeared to-day. Never mind!
I'll do what I can."

Swiftly, deftly, with sterilized water and
antiseptic bandages, she proceeded.

Then came another knock and a bold foot-
step. Luciyeh glanced up and was overjoyed
at seeing Dr. David, a Syrian member of the
college medical staff.

"Mrs. Fitz-Gerald sent me to help you," he
said, throwing off his coat. "Where is the
anesthetic?"

With sense of infinite relief, Luciyeh took her place at his side.

Before the first patient was bandaged, a second was brought, and a third, and another and still others. The whole day the Christian nurse and the Christian doctor worked together under the Turkish flag.

In the evening, when the doctor had left, Luciyeh sent to the hospital board for a military guard, which was promised, but never came. Alone she cared for her patients, never knowing what the mob might do. The God in whom she trusted was shielding her, through the vigilance of a wise city governor, set there in his great providence for this time of need.

A few at a time, during the next day, most of the terrified inmates of the hospital returned, except the prisoners. And Luciyeh's work went on.

The visitor who knows where to seek her may find her to-day, still soothing and restoring with her hand, and inspiring hope and courage from her brave heart.

XVI

TRANSPLANTED
CHILDREN

I

IT was a pretty trick," said Amr Afendeh
Hashim, complacently rolling a cigaret.

He had pulled off his European shoes,
when he returned from his business down in
the old city, and now he was enjoying home
comfort, sitting cross-legged on the divan, even
though his well-fitted European clothes were
stretched in adapting themselves to his Asiatic
pose.

"How did he manage it?" asked the Afendeh's wife, Sitt Habubah, fat and complacent,
in pink calico wrapper, blowing a stream of
bubbles through her argileh.

"It was this way," said her husband, pressing off the ashes of his cigaret upon a carved brass receiver. "You know my brother Selim can outwit the Sheitan! When we sent him to England after the death of our poor brother Abd-Allah over there, he knew very well that we did not want to be bothered with Abd-Allah's young English wife. What a brother of ours wanted with a foreign wife I can't imagine!"

"Such ways!" snorted Sitt Habubah. "She probably walked into the reception-room like a brazen-faced hussy, without a veil, and shook hands with her husband's gentlemen visitors!" The argileh was boiling now with her indignant whiffs.

"Well, Selim was not to be caught," said Amr. "But he knew that, aside from the capital that Abd-Allah left in his business, his two children, Hanifeh and Khudr, were all that was left to us here in Syria to remind us of our beloved youngest brother," and Amr's voice was husky with genuine emotion. "Selim kept on good terms with the English wife," he continued, "until he had wound up Abd-Allah's affairs to the advantage of his brothers in Syria.

Then he told her that he was going to take the children out to smell the air. He did it indeed, taking them to the ship and sailing off with them to Syria! The Englishwoman must have had a good surprise to find herself left alone! And Selim and the children arrive here to-morrow! His letter has come only one day sooner than he himself."

"We can bundle them in with the rest of the children," said Sitt Habubah; "two more will not make much difference when we have the families of you three brothers here already."

Early the next morning, the entire complex household was in great excitement. The ship had been sighted rounding the point, and the two brothers, Amr and Husein, were off to the Port to meet the returning brother Selim and the little niece and nephew. They all came back in a carriage to the house.

The harim crowded each other in the court to get the first glimpse. There were the three wives of the brothers, the aged mother of the family and two unmarried sisters, besides two servant-women who mingled with the rest on familiar terms. All had to restrain their eager-ness in greeting the returning travelers and had drawn veils over their faces, on account of the porters who were carrying baggage into the house. But when Selim Hashim actually stepped into the court, his wife raised the cry of rejoicing, the zlaghit, joined by a chorus of all the younger women, "la-la-la-la-la-la-li!" "For shame! for shame!" cried the quavering voice of the aged mother, "to rejoice over one brother, when the other lies in his grave in a distant land," and tearing open the neck of her dress, she beat her clenched hands upon her bony breast, and chanted the funeral cry for Abd-Allah, the departed.

But the children of the family were not to be restrained. They were everywhere, under foot, five children of Amr, three of Selim and four of Husein, besides the babies carried in the arms of Selim's and Husein's wives. They clutched at their uncle Selim's baggage, demanding insistently where he had put the presents for them.

While Selim's attention was given to his own family, all the rest of the children found wonderful entertainment inspecting the new little cousins. The newcomers stood, timid and bewildered by the jangle of questions hurled

at them in Arabic, which they could not understand. Hanifeh, five years old, looked out
shyly from large black eyes, like those of her
cousins staring at her, and her black hair hung
in heavy curls round her shoulders. But her
three-year-old brother, stocky and closely knit,
with copper-tinted hair, frank blue eyes, and
freckled nose, was as incongruous a bearer
of the name Khudr as could possibly be im-
agined.

What interested the Syrian cousins far more
than the newcomers themselves, was the flaxen-
haired doll which Hanifeh clasped. They fin-
gered its face and hair, and inspected each
article of its clothing with delight, imparting
sundry finger-marks. The older girls were
pulling at Hanifeh's coat and turning up the
corners to feel the silk lining.

One boy snatched Khudr's broad-brimmed
straw hat from his hand, as the little fellow
had pulled it off on entering the house. "Why
don't you wear a hat on your head, in the place
where a hat ought to be?" jeered the older
boy, setting the hat on his own head over his
red fez and proceeding with a mock parade
round the court. Another child gave a tweak

to one of Hanifeh's curls and ran off convulsed with laughter.

"W'low! you young Bedouins!" roared uncle Amr, cuffing the heads of one or two of the nearest ones, who ducked and hovered about just out of reach.

As soon as the uncle's attention was diverted, another boy seized Khudr's patent leather belt with a sudden pull that would have thrown him over, but for Hanifeh's catching him. Finding Hanifeh off her guard, two or three others jerked the doll out of her arms and ran off with it. Little Khudr's blood was up. Planting his two sturdy legs apart, with truly British defiance, he leveled a fat fist square in the nose of the nearest marauder. Howls rent the air.

"Khudr! you bad boy!" cried Selim Afendeh in English, boxing the child's ears, "haven't I told you all the voyage you were like your mother's people!"

"My name is not Kooder," retorted the child stoutly, pronouncing the name with an English accent; "my mother always called me George."

"Khudr is the name your father gave you

and that's your name here," answered uncle
Selim shortly.

Hanifeh's wails were now clamorous:
"Who's got my doll?"

Several children at the end of the court were
contending for it.

"You afrits," cried uncle Selim, "give that
to me!" He pulled the doll away, but already
the top of its head had been broken off, as
though the poor thing had been scalped. He
brought it to Hanifeh, who held out her arms
to it sobbing, as a mother might receive her
wounded child.

"Come now, you must kiss your grandmother's hand," said uncle Selim, taking
Hanifeh and Khudr to the elderly lady, "you
must call her Sit-ty." Rather awkwardly, the
two children obeyed their uncle's command
and kissed the old lady on the back of the
hand.

She took hold of Khudr by the shoulders:
"Can this be my Abd-Allah's son?" Tears
streamed down her withered cheeks. "Let me
smell of you." She pinched his cheek hard,
while drawing a long whiff through her nos-
trils, then making as though she were drawing

away a handful of his cheek, she kissed her closed fingers.

"You hurt!" cried Khudr, drawing away. He soon learned that this was Sit-ty's way of showing her affection, and he submitted with rather poor grace.

"Now you children must behave while the gentlemen eat breakfast," cried Sitt Habubah.

The veiled maid-servants were taking dishes of food into the dining-room.

"Cheer up!" Hanifeh whispered to her afflicted doll; "we'll have something to eat anyway." She started following the men to the breakfast-table, but was promptly pulled back by uncle Selim's wife. She soon realized that the gentlemen ate in state, while their wives and servants waited on them and the children clamored in the kitchen, seizing pieces of flat Arabic bread with a few olives or some cheese, to munch as they roamed around, getting in the way of the women who served.

When the men had finished their breakfast, the women took their turn, the children gathering round their respective mothers, who fed them liberally. Sit-ty saw to Hanifeh and Khudr. They rather liked the bread, which was torn off in pieces, like scraps of tough blotting-paper, and used as a scoop for the prepared food, but the bowls of loppered milk, called leben, they would have none of.

After breakfast, the Hashim brothers went down town. Hanifeh and Khudr gazed tearfully after uncle Selim, as the last link with the life that they knew.

"Shu haida! (What is this!)," cried Sitt Habubah, *"taou!"* They inferred that the word meant "come," and they followed her into a bedroom, where she made them take off their shoes and gave them their choice of an array of house footwear, heelless slippers, black and red, and *kub-kubs,* a wooden sole raised on blocks under the heel and toes and held on by a leather strap over the toes. These novelties attracted them at once, though their cousins seemed to prefer slippers. Clump! clump! clump! they toddled noisily and awkwardly over the marble floor, as though just learning to walk. The cousins roared with laughter and quickly shuffling out of their slippers and sliding their toes into the kub-kubs, they began executing fancy maneuvers, to the mortification of the newcomers. By dint of practise,

Hanifeh and Khudr soon gained skill, and before long they were clumping about with the rest. When this entertainment palled, they wandered back into the rooms and found a charming pastime blowing bubbles into Sitt Habubah's argileh.

At bedtime the greatest surprise of the day came when the maids spread out on the floor a quantity of pallets, which had been folded and piled up at one end of a big room, and the various children disposed themselves upon them, taking off only their dresses and sleeping in their underclothes. The high bedsteads, with silk quilts and mosquito-nets, were for the grown people.

The next day the women were very busy preparing food, elaborate concoctions of dough with spiced dressing rolled in it. In the courtyard, the servant-maids, in full Turkish trousers and skirts tucked up around their waists, pounded meat and wheat into a pulp which they spread in huge flat pans, putting in a layer of chopped meat, onions and pine-cone seeds. They called it *kibbeh*. Throughout the preparations, Hanifeh frequently caught the word "Ramadan."

"What does 'Ramadan' mean?" she asked uncle Selim when he came home in the evening. "That is the month of the great Feast," he said, "when we fast all day and eat at night."

That evening the children were put to bed as before, but at midnight were aroused by a great din outside, a drum and a man's voice calling. All the family jumped up, putting on their outer garments. Lamps were lighted, and maids and matrons together proceeded to serve the elaborate dinner that had been prepared the day before. It was topped off with a generous tray from the confectioner's, puff-paste stuffed with chopped nuts and honey. All the children were frantic with excitement. When the men had feasted and settled down to cigars and argilehs, the women and children partook. The viands were tasty and very rich. Hanifeh and Khudr found their prejudices disappearing and tucked in their good share, though they balked at cucumber salad with loppered milk sauce. They were through perhaps by three in the morning, and all burrowed under their quilts again for a few hours of fitful sleep. The cold gray dawn stole through the round sky-light windows below the ceiling, and Hanifeh and Khudr opened their eyes to gaze forlornly at each other. Oh, such feelings inside them! They were both wretched and could do nothing all day but lie on the floor. The gentlemen went off without breakfast and the harim neither ate, drank, nor smoked the whole day, and the children were given only pick-up lunches of bread and cheese.

At certain hours of the day Sit-ty would spread a rug on the floor and go through a wonderful series of prayers, alternately standing, kneeling, touching the floor with her forehead, and at one point spitting at the Devil!

When the time came for the sunset feast, the cousins were as ready as ever, but Khudr and Hanifeh sickened at the sight. Pale and tearful, they crawled to a corner of the divan and cried themselves to sleep, hugging the broken doll between them.

The month dragged on, the nights being turned into day with feasting, and the days of fasting spent in preparing for the nights. The family all felt cross and Hanifeh and Khudr were sick most of the time.

"I've had my fill of those children!" exclaimed Sitt Habubah, once more seated be-

fore her lord, with her argileh, at the close of
the sunset feast. "Everything goes wrong with
them. We can't understand their language
and they can't understand ours. They forget
to take off their shoes when they come into
the house, and catch cold when they wear kub-
kubs. They are always blowing into my argileh, and they don't get on with our children.
They don't like our food, and when they eat
it they are sick. They cry all the time, but
what more could we do for them?"

Amr Afendeh nodded slowly. "We brothers
have been talking about it. They certainly
don't fit in here. I will take them to-morrow to
Miss Wheeler's school. She can manage
them."

"Anything to get rid of them!" exclaimed
Sitt Habubah.

II

The next day, Hanifeh and Khudr were
again dressed in their best clothes and taken
in a carriage through the narrow streets to the
heavy green-painted gate that led into Miss
Wheeler's mission school.

They were both pale and frightened when Amr Afendeh took them up the stone steps into the garden, bright with early spring flowers.

Miss Wheeler met them at the door-step.

"My dear children, how glad I am to see you," she said in English, in a gentle mother voice, kissing them both.

The pent-up feelings of many weeks broke forth; as though by one instinct, both children seized her round the neck and covered her with kisses.

"For shame!" said Amr Afendeh.

"Never mind," said Miss Wheeler; "I love children."

She led them across the court into a room filled with pictures and home-like looking things, such as the children's mother used to have about her.

After staying long enough for the necessary business arrangements, Amr Afendeh arose and held out the back of his hand to each of the children. They kissed it, as they had been taught to do, and he said good-by.

Miss Wheeler sat down in her wicker arm-chair and opened her arms to the children.

They needed no further invitation and both climbed to her lap.

"You're just like people at home," said Hanifeh.

"You'll call me George, won't you?" said Khudr.

"I'll call you Georgie," answered Miss Wheeler.

"And you have a kitty too!" cried Hanifeh, darting under the divan.

"There comes dear Rudha, who will help take care of you," said Miss Wheeler; "each of our big pupils takes care of one or two little ones."

Rudha stood in the doorway, with a long white veil over her head, hanging each side of her face.

"Welcome to you," she said shyly. Her voice was low and gentle; she spoke English with a sweet modulation, and her lustrous brown eyes smiled upon the children with the same kind of love that looked out from Miss Wheeler's quiet gray ones.

"Come and wash your hands for afternoon tea," said Rudha.

Afternoon tea! Could there be more of a

home touch! They skipped joyfully after her into a long room with rows of water-taps and basins.

"This is where the girls wash," said Rudha. "Miss Wheeler is very particular about our bathing."

Hands washed and hair brushed, they were taken back into the sitting-room, where as a special privilege they were invited to join Miss Wheeler and the teachers. They sat in little chairs, one on each side of Miss Wheeler, and had cambric tea and bread and marmalade, just as they used to have at home.

Rudha took them to the school yard after that, where the white-veiled girls were swinging, playing circle games, or tending the vegetable garden.

They clustered round the new children, questioning them in English.

"What's the matter with your doll?" said a big girl. "Let me make a hood for her and cover the broken head," and she brought from the house some scraps and sewing materials.

"Come, Georgie, let me swing you," said Rudha, and the delighted child found himself swinging back and forth to a sort of chant,

which one girl would sing, all the others joining in the refrain: "Yah! Yah!"

They had supper with the girls at a long
table, plain fare, but eaten with thanksgiving
and good cheer.

"Now we'll have our evening hymn. What
shall we sing?" asked Miss Wheeler.

A chorus of voices said, "Jesus loves me."

"That is good," said Miss Wheeler, "but
this time, we'll let Hanifeh choose her favorite
hymn. What would you like to sing, dearie?"

"I'd like, 'Where are you going, my pretty
maid?' " said Hanifeh promptly. Some of the
children tittered, others looked shocked.

"I mean some hymn, something you sang at
Sunday-school," said Miss Wheeler.

"I didn't go to school on Sundays. That
day we used to go to the Zoo."

Rudha and the older girls looked at each
other amazed.

"We'll sing 'Jesus loves me,' " said Miss
Wheeler quickly to divert attention. "Don't
you know that?"

"No, I never heard it," said Hanifeh simply.

Miss Wheeler played the piano and the children sang heartily. After the second verse,

Hanifeh and George found themselves joining with the rest of the children in the chorus: "Yes, Jesus loves me."

"Now it's time to go to bed," said Miss Wheeler to the two children. "Come this way; I have put two cribs for you right here in my room—I can't put such babies into the dormitory!" she added to herself.

"Oh, we haven't slept in cribs since we left mamma," exclaimed Hanifeh.

"Now we'll say our evening prayers," said Miss Wheeler.

"Do you mean the way Sit-ty does? I can show you how she goes!" cried George.

"No, dear," said Miss Wheeler, "you are both going to kneel down here at my knees and ask dear God to bless you."

"We don't know how," faltered Hanifeh awestruck; "you'd better excuse us."

"You poor little heathen from Christian England!" murmured Miss Wheeler under her breath. Then to the children, "This time, I'll kneel down with you and say the words for you."

She knelt before the white crib, an arm around each child.

"Dear Jesus, who used to be a little boy, take care of little George and Hanifeh to-night and may they learn to love thee, and bless mama so far away, and bless Rudha and the schoolgirls and the teachers——"

"And bless the kitty," prompted George.

"Yes, God will take care of the kitty," answered Miss Wheeler soberly.

The good-night kisses left Miss Wheeler's hair disheveled. "I'm afraid they will get to love me more than they love their mother," she thought, while something caught at her throat.

The next day, she made a call on the household of Amr Afendeh.

"Have you a picture of the mother of Hanifeh and Khudr?" she asked casually.

"Why, yes, our poor Abd-Allah sent it to us when he betrothed her and it has been thrown aside somewhere." After a search among tightly crammed bureau-drawers, the photograph was found.

Miss Wheeler gazed at the vapid face, the conspicuous arrangement of hair. "Do you care for this? May I take it to the children?" she asked.

"Oh, we don't want it; the Kurd take it!" said Sitt Habubah.

Miss Wheeler turned the picture over and read: "Gladys Jenkins, 21 Hawthorne Road, Heathcote."

That evening, when the children went to bed, Miss Wheeler produced the photograph. "Do you know who this is?" she asked.

"Why, it's mama!" they exclaimed.

"She came for you to kiss her good-night," said Miss Wheeler.

A moist kiss was printed upon the picture by each little mouth. This became the nightly custom.

That evening, Miss Wheeler wrote a letter to Mrs. Gladys Jenkins Hashim, 21 Hawthorne Road, Heathcote.

Happy weeks flew by. Hanifeh and George, seated on benches with the infant class, were learning to read from the primer, and could recite many sweet Bible verses both in English and Arabic. They could tell a number of beautiful and wonderful stories about Jesus and they had gained quite a repertoire of hymns, from which they could call for their favorites at evening prayers. Incidentally they had unlearned some spicy profanity that they had picked up from their cousins.

One evening, when they had kissed their mother's picture good night, Miss Wheeler said, "I have something beautiful to tell you. Dear mama is coming on the steamer to-morrow morning!"

"Is it God who's bringing her?" asked George.

"Yes, it is," said Miss Wheeler. "How much we shall thank him!"

At sunrise the next morning, the usual hour for the arrival of steamers, Miss Wheeler went to the landing to meet Gladys Hashim. The schoolgirls waited in a buzz of excitement, peering over the garden wall down into the street. It was an incongruous pair that finally alighted at the gate, Miss Wheeler in her quiet gray suit and the dashing-looking stranger in the extreme of showy fashion.

Hanifeh and George rushed down the steps and threw themselves into their mother's arms. Gladys gathered them to her heart, sobbing, "I didn't think I'd ever see you again."

It was a day of tearful joy. The three could not bear each other out of their sight.

Every few minutes one or the other of the children would run across the room and seize their mother around the neck, while the elaborate coiffure was disarranged and forgotten.

"I will go to-day to see the Hashim brothers," said Miss Wheeler. "I am not going to send the children away by the same kind of a trick which brought them here. They shall be given back to their mother in a perfectly open way."

She returned after a long absence, looking sad. "They will not hear of it," she said; "we shall need patience." They prayed about it that night at family prayers with the girls and beside the white cribs. Miss Wheeler had a way of praying about everything and a way of waiting afterward for the answer, and there was a marvelous sequence which had gradually become familiar to the girls, that the things Miss Wheeler asked for by and by came to pass. Gladys Hashim listened in wonder. This missionary woman talked to God as though he were in the next room and she seemed quite indifferent as to how he would answer, for the certainty that he would bring the right thing to pass was absolute with her.

Miss Wheeler did not embarrass Gladys by
asking her to choose a hymn, but a hymn-book
was handed to her, and as the sweet words
floated upward from the circle of white-veiled
girls, Gladys found the music blurred before
her, and, once and again, heavy tears splashed
down upon the page.

"I incline to take you with me to see the
Hashims," said Miss Wheeler the next morning; "it may emphasize the justice of your
claim."

"I couldn't stand seeing that Selim again,"
exclaimed Gladys; "he stole away my children!"

"God can help you do what you can't do
alone," said Miss Wheeler softly.

A quick answer rose to Gladys' lips and
stopped there. "I'll go with you," she said.

As the fast of Ramadan was now past and
the evening feasts would be no longer an
obstacle, Miss Wheeler and Gladys went to
call late in the afternoon when the brothers
would be home from business. The door was
opened by the bare-footed maid, with skirt
hitched up as usual over the full Turkish
trousers and tucked into her girdle, but with

her face carefully veiled. She ushered them at once into the reception-room, which she would not have done with Moslem ladies, as the three gentlemen were seated there refreshing themselves with their cigarets.

Selim Afendeh flashed a quick glance at Gladys and insolently blew a cloud of smoke towards her. "I see you had to take an ocean voyage to see me again," he remarked.

Gladys flushed to the roots of her hair, but Miss Wheeler diverted attention by introducing her to Afendehs Amr and Husein.

"This is your sister-in-law, Gladys," she said simply. They bowed and shook hands with Oriental grace.

"May we see the ladies?" asked Miss Wheeler.

"Call the harim!" said Amr Afendeh to the maid, who was still peeking in at the door-way, with her bare shins and veiled face.

In a few moments, Sitt Habubah appeared in her usual pink flowered wrapper, followed by her sisters-in-law, carrying their babies straddling on their hips. After much salaaming, Sitt Habubah asked the ladies, "What will you have, cigarets or argilehs?"

"We are satisfied with your presence," said Miss Wheeler.

"And you drink no smoke at all? Shu haida!"

As the guests remained unpersuaded, the hostesses settled down to encourage the conversational muse with the bubbling of their argilehs. The children, who were giggling behind the maid in the court, began to stream into the drawing-room and finger Gladys' clothes and card-case.

"W'low!" cried Amr Afendeh as usual, "do you want Miss Wheeler to think you are wild beasts?"

"God bless them all," said Miss Wheeler, "but praise to his name, it seems to me you have enough children in the house, and could spare Hanifeh and Khudr to go back to their mother."

"Children are the blessing of the Lord," said Amr Afendeh piously; "never would it be possible for us to send away our brother's children. Our house is open; we are ready to receive Sitt Gladys into our harim; let her assume the izar on the street like our ladies and she may be one of us."

Gladys shuddered. "Oh, I couldn't breathe through all that covering. I'd smother!"

Fortunately, candied apricots and sherbet made a digression, and Miss Wheeler turned the conversation into more general topics. They parted on pleasant terms, but no nearer a settlement than before.

"They'll never let the children go," moaned Gladys on the way home; "I can run away with them, as Selim did."

"Not while you are in my home," said Miss Wheeler, kindly but firmly.

Again that evening, she prayed as before.

Gladys came to have a very heavy heart as the weeks went by and Miss Wheeler returned from her periodic visits to the brothers unsuccessful.

The older girls gathered round Gladys on the playground with tender-hearted sympathy over her grief. Everything about her was interesting to them, her clothes, her blooming complexion, her home in the far-away land. They plied her with questions, with their pretty foreign accent. She in turn questioned them.

"Are you girls all from Moslem homes?"

"Yes," they said, "either Moslem or Druse."

"What is Druse?" she asked.

"Oh, that's another sect of Moslems," they answered.

"But you are not like those people at the Hashim house," said Gladys, "and all these little schoolgirls are not the remotest bit like those wild children."

"That is because Miss Wheeler has taught us," said Rudha loyally. "Miss Wheeler is an angel."

"But how did your parents come to send you to the school?" asked Gladys.

"Why, they saw other children who had been to the school and when they realized how much better they behaved and how well they could read and write and sew, besides many other things, they wanted their daughters to be taught too."

"What makes you love Miss Wheeler so much?" she asked, to see what they would say.

She was taken aback by Rudha's answer: "I think it is because she is like the Lord Jesus."

Gladys felt an old resentment rising in her. "What do you care about Jesus? Aren't you Moslems!"

A shocked expression passed over all their faces. "Don't you love the Lord Jesus?" they asked almost with one voice.

Gladys turned upon her heel and went into the house.

The girls looked at each other with tears in their eyes.

"Let's go and ask Miss Wheeler about it," said Rudha. They found their teacher in her flower-garden.

"Miss Wheeler." they asked, "isn't everybody in England a Christian?"

Miss Wheeler was startled and a great pain seized her heart. How could she answer them?

"Dear girls, I wish they were all Christians, but I am sorry to say they are not—all."

"We thought they were all like you teachers," Amineh said sadly, "but we've been talking with the mother of the little children," speaking of her by the title they had all given her, "and we find," her voice dropped, *"she doesn't love the Lord Jesus!"*

"What can we do about it?" asked Rudha.

"What have you learned to do about difficulties?" said Miss Wheeler.

"We'll go and think about it," said Amineh.

Later on, they came back to Miss Wheeler.

"We've decided what we're going to do," said Rudha. "We older girls are going to have a little prayer-meeting every day at the noon recess and pray that God will open the heart of the mother of the little children and teach her to love the Lord Jesus Christ."

More weeks dragged slowly by. An indescribable something was borne in upon Gladys. It came to her in the morning when she bent her head with the girls for a blessing on their simple breakfast; it came to her in the prattle of her own children and their long recitals of Bible stories; it came again at the evening prayer, with the ever-repeated petitions for her and her children; and most of all, it came when her children of their own accord knelt at her knee at bedtime.

One day Miss Wheeler returned from her oft-repeated visit to the Hashim brothers with a radiant face.

"Quick!" she said to Gladys, "they say you can go! They say I have worn them out and they can't stand it any longer! There is a steamer leaving at noon to-morrow. Get ready in a hurry and we'll take you down."

As one in a dream Gladys threw her clothes and her children's into her trunk. There was much exchange of affectionate farewells with the girls, a tearful thanksgiving at prayers after the long beseeching, a sleepless night, and the next morning, Gladys and the children, Miss Wheeler and her associate teacher, all went down to the steamer.

Once on deck, the noise and bustle of a journey about her, she could finally realize that she and her children were free!

Miss Wheeler put an arm about her waist. "Come away with me," she said, "behind the pilot-house; I want to tell you something."

There in that quiet spot, both gazing down through the peerless blue of the water, she told Gladys how the dear circle of girls had been praying every noon day after day for her, that she might come to love the Lord Jesus.

Gladys was choked with sobs.

"Now we must leave you," she said; "the visitors' bell is ringing."

Hanifeh and George ran to Miss Wheeler and clung to her neck.

"How can we thank you enough!" said Gladys.

The visitors were hurried down the gang-
way and the little boat speedily carried them
farther and farther away. Gladys, with her
children beside her, looked over the shining
blue of the bay, on the one hand to the opal-
tinted range of Lebanon, on the other to the
many-colored houses of the city, interspersed
with the green of gardens and palms.

Up in the most thickly-built section, she
could locate the school, so full of new and living experiences for her. While she gazed, the
ship's signal was given for the change of
watch, and she counted, eight bells! noon!
And across the water, she could see, in imagi-
nation, the white-veiled schoolgirls coming out
of their classes for the noon recess, and out
from among them separated that special group
who went by themselves into a corner of the
garden apart; and in the tremulous light hov-
ering over the city Gladys seemed to see rising
to heaven the prayer for her.